SEQUINS STARDOM AND CHLOE'S DAD

D0262907

SEQUINS STARDOM AND CHLOE'S DAD

John Farman

Piccadilly Press • London

Scene 1

The Kingdom of Joe Derby.
Sunday 4.15 p.m.

ACTION:

'MUM! Have you seen Rover?'

'No, I haven't. I'm fed up looking for your flipping dog. The minute my back's turned, he's out the back door and off down the road. I don't know what he's after.'

Unfortunately, I know only too well what he's after – and it isn't dog biscuits. There's a house down the road where they breed pedigree dogs, and he's always hanging around there with the ladies. I suppose you can't blame him for wanting a bit of posh.

About me. Life's a little tricky at the moment. Lucy, my ex, who everyone agrees is a top babe, turned out to be not my type – good beginning, bad end. After the first couple of dates I found I was running out of things to talk about and that all *she* could or *would* talk about was clothes and boy bands. Anyway, about a month ago, she went and dumped me before I even had a chance to dump *her* and wouldn't have me back for love nor money (not that I tried the latter). Then, just over a week ago, she went and dumped this sixth-form prat called James Burton (the one she dumped me for) and now she's trying to get me back again – bloody cheek! I'm still resisting, but it's ever so difficult. She's dead pretty, with a body to die for.

So why has she suddenly started fancying me again? Apart from my undeniable charm and frighteningly good looks, I reckon it's purely because my best mate Merlin and I made this movie and everyone's talking about it and us. I suppose it's fair to say we're sort of celebrities in Northbridge. Admittedly, Hollywood would have been better, but, as the legendary movie maker Cecil B DeMille probably would have said, you've got to start somewhere.

Our film, *La Maison Doom*, could have been a right carve-up had it not turned out funny. To be honest, we were trying to make a serious piece of modern cinema (ha ha), but according to everyone who saw it, it turned out more like a *Carry On* film. Poor old Merlin, who is not unknown to taking himself rather seriously, still hasn't really got over it.

Talking of movies, I've hardly seen any lately. The video shop where I worked on Saturdays closed down, which means my supply has dried up. Having said that, with everything that's been going on, I wouldn't have had time anyway.

My other big problem is Jade Labardia, one of Merlin's two gorgeous sisters (Sky's the other). She's seventeen, a year older than me, and dangles me on a piece of elastic. One minute I think she's really into me, and the next she treats me like a schoolboy, which, admittedly, I still am.

And my other, *other* big problem is that I haven't actually done it yet – all the way – and she's quite experienced, *or so I'm led to believe*.

Anyway, that's where we all are at the moment.

So where is Rover? That's what I want to know. I need him here, now.

'ROVER!' I shout again. This time, in the distance, I hear the scrabbling of paws on kitchen lino. He bounds up the stairs, through the door and into my kingdom.

'God, Rover, where the hell have you been? You look ghastly. Have you been digging? Don't tell me you've been down the road again. Who was it this time?'

Rover cocks his head to one side and tries to look all innocent-like. Then he licks himself in a way that only dogs can.

'You really are disgusting,' I tell him, 'but well done. I'm pleased that someone's keeping their end up.'

I would carry on talking, but I'm feeling fairly stupid – Rover being a dog and all. I'd like to tell him about my biggest, most humungous dilemma – the one involving Chloe, Merlin's sort-of girlfriend, who's going to be a ballet dancer one day. She rang me about half an hour ago to invite me to her parents' Hallowe'en evening and said she especially wanted me to be there. Then she asked me what I thought about Lucy and everything. She might have just been trying to find out for her best friend, I suppose, like girls do, but I thought I detected something else in her voice.

The trouble is I do actually quite fancy her, in a slim bendy kind of way, but I really can't go behind my best mate's back, can I? He's mad about her, or so he says. Mind you, if she's prepared to go behind *her* best mate's back . . .

I decide to ring Merlin to find out what's going on, so I tap out his personal number. His dad's so rich they've got this sort of switchboard thingy that diverts all the calls to different rooms in their massive house. Here, we've just got a phone at the bottom of the stairs, so anyone can hear what you're saying. I've got a pay-as-you-go phone, but as usual I've already paid and gone.

'Hi Merlin, how's it hangin'?'

'Fab, thanks, I'm just making my costume for Chloe's Hallowe'en do. Are you going to show?'

'Don't really know yet.' (I *do* know, but one must appear cool, mustn't one?)

'Aw, go on, it'll be brill. Her parents have hired that big scary room behind the church. It's her mother's birthday as well, apparently. They're really into culture and music and opera and stuff, so they're having a concert before the piss-up.'

'What sort of concert?'

'They're going to play some of the music her dad's made up – sorry, composed – and Chloe and a couple of her mates are going to dance to it.'

'That doesn't sound too bad,' I say.

'Her mother's got some people from the local theatre group to do the place up sort of spooky. It's all going to be based on a theme of ghosts and things that go bump in the night. I suppose the way I'm describing it sounds pretty crummy . . . Anyway, I've been told I've got to go to the concert bit as well, but most of her other friends, like Lucy, are turning up after at her parents' house.'

'Is that the party bit?'

'Yeah. Look, Joe, you wouldn't come with me, would you – to the concert? I reckon I need a bit of support if I'm going to do culture.'

I thought of Chloe's phone call and felt bad. But, if I'm to be honest, not *that* bad.

'Yeah, all right. It does sound a bit spaz, though. When is it – next Saturday?'

'No, Saturday week, seven-thirty. Look, what are you doing? Why don't you come over? Dad left a few lagers in the fridge.'

Scene 2

The Labardia house.
Sunday 5.45 p.m.

ACTION:

The Labardias live about ten minutes away, in one of the smartest roads in town (if you can call Northbridge a town). Merlin's dad is quite a well-known artist, and he and Merlin's mum and his two sisters, Jade and Sky (and Merlin of course), wallow in crumbly Gothic splendour in a house that makes the one in *Psycho* look like a Barratts show home. By the way, they're all, without exception, totally bonkers and, coming from a dead normal family like mine, I love them to death for it.

Merlin's mum and dad have also just added an entry phone system, because they're dead tired of always having to answer the door for their kids. I push the one with a skull and cross-bones and then climb the twisting staircase to his attic room right under the roof. I tug the bell pull on Merlin's door and wait for it to open.

'Hi Joe, come on in,' he says. 'Park your bum and have a swig.'

I stare at Merlin. He's dressed as a witch, with pointy hat, long flowing green hair (his own) and one of those gruesome rubber witch masks you can get in joke shops. I must admit, I think, for once it's a bit staid for him . . . until he opens his glittery cloak with a flourish. I gasp when I see he's wearing a black sort of basque covered

6

in sparkly sequins, with stockings and suspenders and high-heeled boots.'

'Merlin you prat, you can't go like that. Are you round the bend? You really have gone too bloody far this time. Chloe's parents will go ballistic! I thought you said they were quite posh. Call me old-fashioned, but I think they just might not be that desperate for a sequin-covered transvestite partner for their darling daughter. It was bad enough when you came to your own party as Marlene Dietrich. Go and change, for God's sake – I can't even talk to you like that . . . and I'm *used* to you.'

Merlin shuffles sulkily into the gloomy recesses of his room, muttering obscenities to himself.

His huge attic space is reassuringly the same. Dark as a dungeon, and lit by flickering candles. I notice what look like an extra pair of twinkly eyes staring at me. Let me explain. The Labardias have this thing about pets. From way, way back, any animal belonging to them or their close relatives that dies gets stuffed. I know it sounds weird – even a bit perverted – but it's almost the opposite. The Labardia family love their animals so much they can't bear to part with them, even when they die. I've often wondered why they don't stuff their actual family members when they pass away. I asked Merlin once and he said his mum and dad reckoned it was against the law. I suppose that proves they have thought about it.

'What happened to Denise?' I ask, peering at the new

addition – a small female hare that used to have the run of the house (before being stuffed, that is).

'I'm afraid Dingo finally got her. She was getting a bit slow in her old age.'

Dingo's their big, yellow dog that no one has ever been ever been able to get near to. He prowls around the garden striking terror into all the other animals, domestic or wild, and hardly has to be given any dog food because he finds his own. The story goes that while on holiday in Australia the Labardias rescued him when he was just a sweet little puppy. They found him on the edge of a small town and thought the poor little mite had been abandoned. They're now pretty sure he must have been a wild dog and that his mum had simply left him for five minutes while she killed him something for his tea. So they hadn't rescued the poor little sod at all – they'd kidnapped him! Not only that, but they dragged him back to England and paid for him to be in quarantine for six months. He's certainly never forgiven them, so everyone gets out of his way when they see him coming (apart from Denise, it would appear).

Merlin finally strolls back into view wearing his everyday weird clothes.

'By the way,' I ask, as casually as I can muster, 'how are you getting along with Chloe? You haven't mentioned her lately.'

'Oh, I don't know. I like her lots, but it just doesn't seem to go anywhere, if you know what I mean. We get on great, but just as mates. It never gets remotely physical. I suppose when it comes down to it, she's a bit too skinny for me, and I'm a bit too weird for her. I know what I like about her best of all, though. It's her style. She wears some groovy clothes – just the sort of stuff I'd wear if I was a girl.'

I've never thought about that before. I begin to wonder what I'd wear if I was a girl. Odd thought or what? I suppose if I do think about it, it would be almost the equivalent of how I dress as a bloke. I'd like to be sexy, *naturellement*, but not over-the-top, like Jade is sometimes (not that I'm complaining). I reckon I'd be more like Lucy . . . how can I put it? – a bit more *Sunday Times* than *Mail on Sunday*.

'What are you going to wear to the party?' Merlin asks.

'Oh, you know me. I'll probably just do some token thing – vampire teeth or stitches round my neck. I still can't handle fancy dress. I think it's soppy.'

'Did you know, Chloe's invited Mum and Dad and Sky and Jade. She was round here the other week and they were all going on and on about how much they like dancing. It's a girlie thing, I think. Dad's not so sure, but he'll go anywhere for a drink. So will I, come to that.'

We drink beer and chat away about our next film until eleven or so. Sometimes I stay overnight, but it's a school day tomorrow so I decide to walk home.

Scene 3

Northbridge High School.
Monday 11.35 a.m.

ACTION:

'Derby, might I enquire if there's anyone *in?*'

It's Grunter Griffiths our history teacher, and he's speaking to me.

'In where, Sir?' I answer rather daringly.

'Inside your head, operating your poor excuse for a brain. I just asked you a question.'

'Oh, er, sorry. Could you repeat it? I didn't quite catch the last bit.'

'I'll tell you what,' he says, determined to rub it in, 'You just tell me the part that you did hear, and I'll finish it. I'd hate to have to repeat myself unnecessarily.'

'Was it about Queen Elizabeth, Sir?'

'No, Derby, I was enquiring after Kylie Minogue's bottom. Seeing as the last four periods have been about the Elizabethans, I think it fair to assume that Elizabeth might have come into it somewhere.'

'We'd rather talk about Kylie Minogue's bottom,' yells my mate Spike Davies, mercifully taking the heat off me.

The rest of the class guffaw in best loutish tradition, causing old Grunter to ram a book down on his desk to retain order.

'Labardia, do you know anything particularly interesting about Queen Elizabeth's personal habits? For

Derby's benefit, we were talking about everyday life in 16th century society . . .'

Merlin thinks for a bit then replies. 'Well, she always seems a bit pale, Sir, in all the paintings. Perhaps she didn't eat her greens. Oh yes and she was a virgin all her life, so she never got . . .'

'Thank you, Labardia, I think we get the picture.'

Actually, history's one of my very best subjects and despite this morning's less than sparkling performance, I'd spent quite a lot of time in the library swatting up on the Elizabethans. Not to get into old Griffiths's good books, I might add, but because the whole of that period really turns me on. If ever there's anything on the telly about those times, I can't tear myself away. God knows why.

'She used a sort of foundation make-up made out of white lead, Sir,' I say. 'It was because being pale was reckoned to be cool in those days, a bit like suntans are now. After using it for several years, it ate right into her skin and caused horrible holes like she'd been chewed by rats. She was a right mess, apparently.'

'Is there anything else about her domestic habits that comes to mind?' Grunter asks.

'Well, Sir, this isn't *just* about her, but all posh women in those days used to smother themselves in goose-grease when the weather started to turn chilly and then had themselves sewn into their underwear all through the winter. It was because those great big houses had no central heating. They sometimes didn't have a bath for months and months.'

'Didn't that make them smell rather unpleasant?'

'Yes, Sir, but in those days everyone in court held little bags full of flowers or herbs and stuff under their noses, called nosegays, to hide the pong.'

Poor Grunter looks almost disappointed at my vast knowledge. Before he can even try to embarrass me any further, I'm saved by the break bell.

As we're walking out of the class, Merlin looks a bit puzzled.

'Hey Joe, I've been meaning to ask you, has your dad changed his wheels?'

'No, why?'

'Well I could have sworn I saw your mum in the front seat of a brand new Jag the other night. I was walking back from Chloe's quite late.'

'No way, not in my dad's league,' I say. 'Anyway, Mum's got her own car.'

'I'm sure it was her. Were your mum and dad out on Tuesday night?'

I thought for a bit. This was a bit like being interviewed by Jeremy Paxman or someone.

'Dad was in his shed all evening but Mum did go to some book club thingy she's just joined. She got back quite late. I heard her coming in about eleven-thirty. I know that because that programme about transvestites had just finished.'

'You don't think she's seeing another bloke, do you? I've always thought your mum was nice-looking. I should think lots of men of that age quite fancy her.'

'Don't be bloody daft,' I laughed. 'Mum wouldn't know where to start. Anyway she's far too old for all that stuff. She's gone forty.'

'You're never too old for lurve,' Merlin said sarcastically, throwing his arm round my shoulder, and fluttering his eyelashes. Not long ago, that might have made me laugh, but for some peculiar reason I felt ever so slightly uncomfortable.

My house
4.00 p.m.

When I get home, I can't take my eyes off Mum. It's dead odd. It's as if I'm seeing her for the first time. Jeez, I think, now I've got something else to take up my precious brain space. Up till now she's just been Mum. I've always known she's quite pretty and all that, but I suppose I didn't really think of her as a woman. I never really had to.

Down in the kitchen, having my tea, I start to look at her in a way I never have before. Blimey, Merlin's actually right. My old lady's quite tidy for someone of her age. Come to that, she looks kind of different. She had her hair cut quite recently in a much more trendy way – like that woman on Channel 4 who does the weather. I remember because she had a go at Dad for not even noticing. And come to that, she doesn't look as grey as she used to. She must be dyeing her hair. I can't believe I've not noticed that before either.

'Have you finished, darling?' she says to me. 'There's some chocolate chip ice cream in the freezer. Can you help yourself? I'm out tonight at the Adult Education Centre and I'm a bit late. It's Keep Fit tonight.'

Keep Fit? Since when's she been doing Keep Fit? And why? Dad doesn't care what she looks like, I'm sure. Perhaps it's just to get healthy. I suppose she can't do as much during the day any more, since she's been working in that dress shop in town. Maybe that's why she's been going out so much in the evenings.

About fifteen minutes later she comes down the stairs. For some reason I look up from the telly and watch her fiddling about with her hair in the hall mirror. Normally I'd expect someone going to Keep Fit to be wearing some naff sort of tracksuit or something kind of loose, but Mum's looking quite smart and *not carrying a bag with a towel in*! She's even wearing glossy red lipstick and darkish eyeshadow! I suddenly realise that if I saw her in the street, as a someone I'd never seen before sort of thing, she'd look pretty good. Oh my God. I can't believe this. Don't say I'm beginning to fancy my own mum. The Greeks used to write plays about that sort of stuff . . . I try to get down to my homework, but it's no use – I just can't concentrate. Maybe Merlin was right. Maybe my mum is seeing someone else. I decide, just to put my mind at rest, to bike down to the Adult Education Centre to check for her car.

Fifteen minutes later, I swerve into the car park and clock what's there. Thank God, I can see her red Polo parked on the far side. Jeez, how could I think such a thing of my own mother? I'm just about to cycle home, when I decide to have a pee in the gents just inside the entrance. As I'm coming out, I hear singing coming from the big hall. I look at the programme on the notice board that tells you what goes on, and on which night. It says the Northbridge Choral Society are rehearsing tonight. That's weird, my mum can't sing to save her life. I look down the list for the Keep Fit evening but there doesn't seem to be one. Then, just beside it, I spy this typed note saying that Keep Fit was cancelled a couple of weeks ago, due to the instructor being pregnant. It would all start again, it said, when they found a replacement.

So why was Mum's car here?

Suddenly the light bulb flickers ... and then stays on. Oh my God, that's it! I can't believe it. I bet she meets the bloke in the Jag in the Adult Education Centre car park, and he brings her back after they've been wherever they've been – OR HAVE DONE WHATEVER THEY'VE DONE!

Scene 4

The Labardia house.
Monday 8.12 p.m.

ACTION:

I cycle round to Merlin's – this is an emergency, after all. It's really weird. I've never cared about what my parents got up to. Mum watched her soaps, Dad made his model whatevers in his shed. Every year we'd go to the flipping Lake District or somewhere else just as tedious for our hols and each Christmas the rellies would come round to us on Boxing Day and Dad would get a bit pissed. So it went on – and on . . . and *on*. I suppose, to be honest, I never really wondered whether they were happy or not. I just assumed they were, because they just sort of got on with it.

I think of myself now – aged sixteen, young, ambitious, looking forward to my first proper sexual experience (hopefully with Jade), my first car, my illustrious career in the movies, fame, fortune and all that. I wonder if my dad was ever like that. I wonder if he always wanted to be a quantity surveyor. I wonder if, like me, he ever lost sleep over getting a girl into bed – or lots of girls into lots of beds. If he did, I wonder when it all stopped. Most of all, I wonder when he decided that this was it, or that this was his life – for better or for worse sort of thing. Did he suddenly stop wanting a Porsche or a BMW and did he actually decide a Ford

Orion was all he could expect? Did he actually make up his mind that making model steam engines and smoking illicit fags in his shed with his girlie mags was an acceptable way of spending his evenings?

And what about Mum? . . . I've seen pictures of her when she was young and she was a quite a babe – short skirts, long hair, no bra and all that. I wonder when she decided that she wanted to spend the rest of her life with a bloke like my dad . . . that he was as good as she was ever going to get? I wonder if she ever wanted to be something else more glamorous – like a model or an air hostess or even a lap-dancer (if they had such things in those days).

'Hi Merlin. Look, sorry to come round sort of uninvited, but I think you might have been right about my mum.'

'What about? Oh, that she's seeing another bloke? Oh hell, Joe, sorry I joked about it. I'm sure I'm wrong.'

I told him about the car in the car park and her going out all dressed up for Keep Fit.

'Well, at least he's got a better car than your dad. I quite like the new Jag. It's slightly retro-looking. Whoops, there I go again.'

'Shut it Merlin. This is serious. I could be about to come from a broken home.'

'Hey! That's cool, you could come and live here. There's plenty of room.'

For some reason, I'm not so sure.

'What do you think I should do?' I ask. 'Should I tell

Dad and let him deal with it? Quite honestly, my mum could come in looking like she'd been dragged through a hedge backwards and I doubt if he'd notice anything.'

'You can't. Not until you're sure, anyway.'

'How can I ever be?'

Merlin paced up and down and then went and made a couple of teas in his little kitchen.

'We've got to follow her,' he said when he came back.

'We?'

'You bet, you and me. This is too good to miss. Hey, we could video it.'

'Merlin, this isn't just for your bloody entertainment. This is my mother we're talking about. How would you like it if it was your mum?'

'Don't even go there. I know for a fact my mum and dad were right ravers when they were first married.'

'What – you mean . . . ?'

'According to my sisters, my mum confessed all when they were having girlie talks about not getting pregnant and stuff. They used to go to these parties up in the West End where everything went on, apparently.'

'Like what?'

'Well, you know . . . *everything*.'

'Didn't they mind each other doing it with other people?'

'No way. They used to meet up in the morning and come home together.'

'Do they still do it?' I ask, looking at Merlin in complete shock.

'No way. Not now they're older. Anyway, I think my dad caught something he shouldn't have and that put a stop to it.'

'No wonder you weren't surprised to see my mum.'

'Not at all. Good for her, I say. Your dad's so boring he could play for Tedious United. I always said your mum could be dead gorgeous if she tried. Trouble with you, Joe, is that you don't see her as a real person. I bet you can't bear the idea of her being happy with someone else.'

'I feel like I want to kill the bastard.'

'Why? He's probably got a wife like your dad, if you see what I mean. Nobody takes someone away from someone if they don't want to go. That's bollocks, that is.'

'How do you know all this?' I ask.

'Oh, I don't know. I sometimes feel like I understand women better than men. If you did but know it, your dad might be more frustrated than her. You said you keep finding girlie mags in the shed. The trouble is, he hasn't the balls to do anything about it. He just worships at the shrine of respectability. That's why your mum's made the first move.'

Sometimes Merlin amazes me by just how grown-up he can be. He so often comes across as an immature prat, but underneath there's a whole load of other things going on. So much so that sometimes I don't even understand what he's going on about. He makes me feel like a kid.

'I have to know, Merlin. Then I'll be able to decide whether I should do anything.'

'Right. Next time you know she's going out, why don't we shoot down to the car park and see if this geezer turns up? We can hide in the bushes round the back.'

I feel awful about it, but agree.

Scene 5

The Adult Education Centre car park.
Tuesday 7.30 p.m.

ACTION:

Jeez, it's freezing in these bloody bushes.

Mum said last night that she had to go out tonight to a rehearsal of the pantomime the amateur dramatic society are putting on. Merlin joked that it should be *Jack and the Kama Sutra*, but I thought it in rather bad taste given the circumstances. I find myself hoping and praying that this time the thing's genuine. It's one thing *thinking* your mum's having an affair, but it's another actually *knowing*.

Mum's red Polo swings into the car park and pulls up at the far end where I saw it before. Oh no, just as I suspected, she's just sitting there, touching up her lipstick in the rear-view mirror. A couple of minutes later, Merlin jogs me and I turn just in time to see a flash, silver Jag schmooze in alongside hers. I can't see the driver, but I can tell it's a man – and I can tell it's *not* my dad. I can hardly bear to watch as my mother hops from one car to the other and kisses him full on the mouth, for ages. It looks very much as if tongues might be involved. I feel like I'm going to chuck up and turn away. The Jaguar reverses out and drives right past us. Just as it passes where we're hiding, the security light illuminates the bloke's face. He's quite good-looking –

about my mum's age, with long wavy hair. I suppose you'd call him arty.

When they're gone, I turn to Merlin. Even in the dim light, he looks like he's seen a ghost.

'What's the matter? Do you know that bloke or something?'

He doesn't speak for ages and then says, very slowly, 'You bet I know him, Joey boy. It's Chloe's bloody father!'

'What d'you mean? *Your* Chloe?'

'I can't believe it,' says Merlin quietly. 'I didn't even know they knew each other.'

I rack my brains, but can't come up with the connection. Chloe's not even at our school, so they can't have met at parent-teacher evenings. Anyway, my mum and dad never go to them, or, should I say, I never tell them when they're on.

'Hang on a minute,' says Merlin. 'Chloe told me he's written the music for some local amateur production. A musical. It couldn't be your mum's panto, could it?'

At that moment a couple of people walk from their car and see us sitting in the bushes chatting quietly. They mutter something about there being too much of that sort of thing these days and rush past quickly.

Merlin's dungeon.
8.00 p.m.

Back at Merlin's we try to get our heads round what we've just seen.

22

'Did you say he's a composer or something?' I ask Merlin.

'Yeah. I think he writes advertising jingles for a living, though. Hence the flash car.'

'Blimey, you could put everything my mum knows about music on a pin head.'

'That may be why he fancies her. Opposites attract and all that.'

'Jeez, he couldn't be more opposite to my poor old dad,' I groan.

I start thinking about Chloe's phone call the other week. Talk about messy! There's me fancying a girl whose dad's almost certainly giving my mum one. At this rate, I'll end up being her brother. Jeeeeeesus! If the *EastEnders* writers came up with a plot like this, they'd be shown the bloody door.

'Oh hell's bells,' I say. 'This gets worse. I've just remembered, Mum asked Dad if he'd take her to this concert thingy next week. I was surprised because they never go out. You don't suppose it's the Hallowe'en concert that Chloe's dancing in, do you?'

'Let's face it, sunshine, the way things are going, it's flipping bound to be. Boy oh boy, this is getting interesting. All we need now is for your dad to be having an affair with mine.'

'Your what?' I say grumpily. 'Your mum or your dad?'

Merlin nearly collapses laughing, but I change the subject immediately. I can't even allow my mind to go anywhere near there.

'What the hell am I going to do?' I say. 'I can't go to this thing knowing what's going on. I must admit my mum's got some balls bringing the old man along. It's asking for trouble.'

'Not necessarily,' says Merlin. 'If you think about it, taking him along to her boyfriend's big night is more likely to throw anyone completely *off* the scent, especially your dad. Or . . . it could be that whole thing about wanting to be found out. I read about it in a magazine once. Sometimes people can't bear the deviousness, but haven't got the balls to do anything about it. So they almost flaunt it in front of other people until someone notices.'

'My dad couldn't smell a rat if it was dead for six months and waved in front of his nose. I can't believe Mum's so devious. Jesus, what would my granny have said. I wish she were here now – she'd know what to do.' (My gran died a couple of months ago and I think about her every single day.)

'Knowing her, she'd think it a real laugh. She always thought your dad was a right plonker, didn't she?'

I suddenly feel unbelievably sorry for my old man. I remember the talk we had when I was so upset on the day my gran actually died. He actually admitted how boring and straight he was.

'Do you know, Merlin,' I say, 'I've no idea how my dad would react if he found out. They've been together for ever.'

'Well, sorry mate, but he might have to find out if

24

this goes the distance. Anyway, look on the bright side, she might take you and Rover with her.'

I can't help laughing. You just can't stay serious for long with Merlin around.

Scene 6

The Kingdom of Joe Derby.
Saturday 6.00 p.m.

ACTION:

It's the night of Chloe's dad's Hallowe'en concert and I'm in my kingdom feeling pretty pissed off. In fact, I've been feeling pretty pissed off for the last couple of weeks. Every time my eyes meet Mum's I have to turn away. She must have noticed by now. Dad, of course, blunders on regardless. I sometimes think if she brought her new bloke home and actually did it in the front room he'd hardly notice. It would just be another person on the sofa, as far as he's concerned. I even wonder if he'd mind if he found out Mum was seeing someone else. I reckon, as long as she didn't actually leave him and came back every night to cook his tea and iron his shirts, he wouldn't be too fussed. Still, what do I know?

What I do know is that he's tried everything to get out of going to this flipping concert thingy tonight. He even made out that we couldn't leave Rover and our budgie Tweetie on their own and selflessly volunteered to stay behind. Now I know for sure about Mum and Chloe's dad, I don't feel like going either. It's bad enough going there thinking that Merlin's girlfriend might fancy me, but quite another having to witness my mum and Chloe's dad in the same room, probably eyeing each other up in front of my poor unsuspecting father. But

26

Mum seems determined he should go, and I can't decide which of Merlin's two versions are right. I know my mum's always hated not telling the truth, so I really am beginning to wonder if she wants to bring this whole messy business to a head.

If that isn't enough for one night, on top of all that there'll be the Lucy thing – what a nightmare, with a capital L! She's still phoning up wanting to get back with me, while Chloe, her best friend and Merlin's girlfriend could be wanting to start something up. Then, just to put the bloody tin lid on the whole sorry business, there'll be Jade Labardia, looking as gorgeous as ever, no doubt chatting someone up right in front of me. Sounds like all the makings of a great evening, eh!

At half past six Mum tells Dad to try and look a bit more casual – less straight-looking. It's a bit like asking Kylie Minogue not to look sexy. Dad doesn't really do casual – it's either slobbing-around-at-home clothes or standard office uniform. Poor guy doesn't have a clue and comes down the stairs wearing his navy blue golf club blazer with the Hawaiian shirt my mum bought him on holiday last year. We giggle, and she sends him back and makes him put on the blue shirt he sometimes wears for work, his grey cardigan and a pair of brown corduroys. Now he reminds me of my school caretaker, poor sod. Mum's bought (or borrowed) yet another new dress from where she works and looks more glam than she's ever looked before. Poor old Pa has to be reminded he's still wearing his slippers when we get to the front door. Hell, he's so *un*cool it's almost cool.

'So what's this thing going to be like, Barbara?' he asks for the fiftieth time. 'What sort of music is it going to be?'

'You'll soon find out, Derek. It's very modern and "with it".'

I laugh to myself. My mother wouldn't know modern and "with it" (as she calls it) if it hit her on the back of the head.

'Where have you heard it, dear?' says Dad, totally innocent-like.

Mum hesitates for a fraction of a second. A fraction of a second too long, for my eagle ears.

'Oh er, Gerald (urghh – GERALD!!!) played some of his compositions at one of our music evenings. He's a composer, you know, and an excellent player.'

With whom? I'm tempted to ask.

St Albans Church, Northbridge.
7.15 p.m.

When we arrive at the church, Dad parks his brown Orion right next to Gerald's gleaming silver Jag. If only he knew what had been going on in that car only a night or so ago.

'Nice motor car that,' says Dad. 'I bet that set the bloke who owns it back a few quid. You'll get a smoother ride in that than in any other car – so I've heard.'

Mum looks a bit twitchy and I stare at Dad, who looks completely oblivious.

If a bomb dropped on the church tonight, just about every arty person in the area would be wiped out. Fancy-dress parties only work (if they work at all) if everyone does it. At this one only a few have made the effort. The rest look a bit predictable – all trying to look arty and original, but ending up looking like clones of each other. I glance across at Merlin's parents, who, not to be outdone, have chosen totally over-the-top his-and-her sorceress and wizard outfits. Merlin, despite my protestations, has come in the transvestite witch costume he showed me (without pointy hat), but is thankfully keeping the cloak tightly wrapped round him. Jade and Sky, who couldn't look less than fab if they spent six weeks at an ugly farm, have chosen, for some obscure reason, to be what appear to be Japanese witches with matching black silk kimonos split so low that you could practically see their belly buttons. Needless to say, I'm wearing my new nearly black suit, with a nearly black shirt and a shiny-blue, pencil-thin tie. The only concession I've made to Hallowe'en are two little red tooth marks on my neck. Cool? . . . I think so.

As we are shown to our seats, Gerald (God, how I hate that name), starts fussing around on one side of the raised part of the room with a few other musicians. I must admit he looks quite impressive in a *Phantom-of-the-Opera*-style long purple cloak. I look towards Mum only to see she has a really soppy expression on her face and can't take her eyes off him. I suppose you'd call it love. (Yuck!)

'Ladies and gentleman, witches and warlocks,' he says, attempting a feeble joke in a rather high, rather posh, voice, 'may I welcome you all to our little Hallowe'en concert. The pieces I have composed are based on the text of *Macbeth,* by the great bard William Shakespeare. My daughter Chloe and a few of her friends from ballet school will provide some movement to accompany the work. I do hope you will enjoy it. Afterwards, perhaps you'd like to join Cynthia and myself at our home just round the corner for Hallowe'en drinks.'

I look round the hall, taking in all the people who seem really turned on by the prospect. As the lights dim, Gerald starts tinkling on one of the high notes up the right-hand end of the piano and the bloke on the cello has a go at plucking all the strings at once, as fast as he can. A scary woman with red spiky hair, who looks like a refugee from a Hammer film, bashes a load of little gong things in no apparent order and a bloke on a trumpet makes a noise like a freshly strangled cat. I think at first they're tuning up, but after about ten minutes, I realise this might actually be it. So, apparently, does my dad.

'They'd better be careful, or they might accidentally break into a tune,' he whispers, making me giggle. Suddenly from the wings, three girls, dressed as sort of scantily clad witches or nymphs, leap in and start prancing about like nobody's business. I recognise Chloe instantly and think how fit she looks with not much on. I know I don't know much about modern dance, or modern women come to that, but I know fit when I see it. Legs that go on and on for ever, a body that would cause the makers of slimming pills to go bust, not to mention small but beautifully formed boobs with nipples apparent – what more could a sex maniac like me want? But it's her face that takes my breath away. Usually Chloe doesn't wear a trace of make-up, but this time she's wearing the full works, and with her long reddish hair piled up on top and tumbling around her face in sparkly tendrils, she's transformed into the most beautiful young babe – right up there with Jade and Sky. She reminds me a bit of that gorgeous, tall, freckly girl in that appalling Irish 'Riverdance' thing (the one where they used to prance around without using their arms).

The girls dance brilliantly, considering how bloody awful the music is. It sounds like the sort of stuff Melvyn Bragg sometimes has on the *South Bank Show* – all plinky-plonky and scratchy, without any sign of anything you can tap your foot to or whistle afterwards. Even the trying-to-look-arty audience looks confused and several clap at the wrong places and then look embarrassed. I can hear Merlin giggling in the row behind me. Mum has that sort of I-know-it-must-be-good-but-I-can't-quite-get-my-head-round-it expression, while Dad slips out to the toilets for a sneaky fag. I know my parents so well.

But I can't take my eyes off Chloe. From the rather shy, skinny girl who seemed happy to walk in Lucy's admittedly babe-ular shadow, she's now in complete control. Her slender body does things that mine hasn't even thought of and I reckon her performance dominates everyone else's. Just as she's writhing around in one of the slow bits, she catches my eye and gives me a look that, if I'd done it to her, would have had me arrested. Just to the right, in the row in front of me, Jade catches it (she misses nothing) and throws me a little knowing smile. I look back at her with a dumb, 'who-me?' expression, like the smaller of the two blokes in Laurel and Hardy (I never know which one is which), but I'm sure it didn't convince anybody.

Jade floors me. One minute she's telling me how much she fancies me and snogs me to within an inch of my life, and the next she's almost encouraging me to chase other girls. What's that all about? Maybe by smiling, as she did just then, she's covering her rampant jealousy. Then again – maybe not!

The music (for want of a better word) finally stops and the audience, in its best emperor's-new-clothes manner, claps deliriously, none of them wanting to be suspected of not understanding. When it dies down Chloe, looking flushed and fantastic, runs straight up to me.

'Hi Joe. It's great you could come. What did you think?'

'Brilliant,' I say, 'I didn't really get what the band

were up to, but you were fab.' (I could have kicked myself for calling it a band.)

'Are you coming to the party at our house? It's only round the corner. I think your mother and father are.'

I nearly say, 'You can bet your leotard my mother is,' but think better of it.

Merlin walks over, not the least bit miffed that Chloe came to me first. He's so cool.

'Blimey, Chlo, I thought you were going to end up in knots. I bet some of those positions could come in very useful.'

Chloe glowers at Merlin and goes even redder than she is already. 'Well you're never going to find out, *are* you?' she replies haughtily. 'Anyway, why would you be interested? – you're dressed as a woman, unless I'm mistaken.'

'Yeah, but I can turn myself into anything I want.'

'Well turn yourself into a Coke. I'm dead thirsty.'

Merlin absolutely loves these back and forth exchanges with Chloe, and, like her, never really takes offence. They've been going on like that since they first met.

I'm still standing by my mum and dad when Chloe turns to me again.

'Joe, have you met my father?'

'Er no, I'd like to,' I lie, 'but he looks far too busy to . . .'

She pulls him away from another couple. 'Daddy, this is Joe Derby, he's the one that made the film with Merlin.'

33

A slightly defensive look crosses his face when he realises who I am, but he covers it well. 'I've heard it's very funny . . . well done,' he says pleasantly, 'and these must be your parents.'

Jeeeeez, cool or what, I think. Mum looks as if her dress has opened down the front and stutters, 'Yes, I believe we've already met.'

'I'm Joe's dad,' says Dad. 'How d'you do? Tell me, do you do that sort of music for a living?'

Chloe's father laughs amiably and just a little patronisingly. 'I'm afraid not. I'm forced to work in the wicked world of advertising to earn my meagre crust. I write music for TV ads.'

'Well, you must be doing all right to have a motor like that.'

Mum, Gerald and I give Dad the strangest look. How the hell did he know it was his car?

At that moment, Chloe's mum, a rather horsey-looking woman with large striped satin boobs, runs over to join us.

'Gerald darling, you know you haven't got time to chatter.' She gives him an admonishing wag of the finger, neighs loudly, and all of a sudden we all know who wears the trousers in the house we're about to go to. 'We have to go back to welcome our guests. Now, do come along.'

Scene 7

Chloe's house.
Saturday 8.45 p.m.

ACTION:

Why do I only seem to know people with far more money than me? Chloe's place is one of those detached houses covered in beams and stuff, which makes it look much older than it really is. Naff but pricey. There's a crunchy, tree-lined drive leading to the doorway, and what appear to be a couple of waiters standing just inside with trays of drinks.

'Blimey,' whispers Dad. 'If I'd known it was going to be like this I'd have worn smarter trousers.'

Suddenly I feel an overwhelming rush of affection for my old man – and a new respect. Whether or not that was a clever guess about the Jag, I thought he was handling all this with just the seriousness it deserved . . .

Mum scans the place in awe – probably wondering what it would be like to clean it if and when she moves in. Dad's now enjoying making me laugh and turns to one of the men with drinks and asks if the place has an inside loo. I practically wet myself and suddenly need a loo myself. There's something different about my dad tonight. Something I haven't seen before. Normally he wouldn't dream of taking the piss or doing anything that might cause a scene. I really wonder if he knows all about the wonderful Gerald and Mum and has some sort of strategy. After the loo, instead of rushing off, as I would normally have done, I hang around my dad to see what's going to happen.

'Joe, sweet, you're here at last. I was beginning to give up on you.'

It's Lucy looking cool and sexy in a long Cruella DeVille-type black dress with loads of dangly bits and split right up to the thigh. She's wearing her hair curly – a bit Page 3, but hey! Across the room, I see her mother, in a long black wig and, under a floaty sort of cloak, a body-stocking so tight that it practically shows anyone who cares to look hard enough how much she had for lunch. What a pair! (I mean Lucy and her mum.)

'Hi, Luce, you look fab,' I say. She kisses me and then turns to Dad.

'Hello, Mr Derby. Remember me?' she says, with a flirty flutter of the eyelashes.

Poor Dad, who's only just managed to tear his eyes away from Lucy's mother, can hardly speak. 'Oh, hello Lucy dear,' he gulps. 'We haven't seen you for ages. When are you coming round again? We miss you.'

'Oh, whenever Joe asks me, I suppose. I'm afraid he doesn't love me any more.' She then puts on one of those little-girl-lost faces guaranteed to score maximum points.

I'm just about to remind her that *she* actually dumped *me*, when I notice my mum and the wonderful Gerald talking earnestly in the doorway. He looks as if someone's just told him that his old chap's hanging out.

I bet it's got something to do with what my dad said about the car. Dad, on the other hand, seems to be really enjoying himself. He's now chatting away with Chloe ten to the dozen. When they stop, and he goes off to find another drink, she comes over to me.

'You never told me about your dad,' she says.

'Told you what? There's not much to tell – unless I've missed something.'

'He's one of the most unpretentious people around. He told me he thought the dancing was great, but the music sounded as if had been composed at a school for the deaf. He said that he didn't understand it at all.'

'That doesn't necessarily make it bad, though,' I say, trying rather poncily to make excuses for my own dad.

'No, it doesn't. But I think you should never go along with what everyone else thinks. He said that he was sorry that it was my father who'd composed it, but he thought it was rubbish, and it would stay rubbish until anyone could persuade him different. Don't you think that's brave, Joe?'

I could say that he might have had other reasons for hating it, but decide against it.

Chloe takes me to one side. 'Joe, I've been wanting to talk to you. Could we go into the hall?'

Oh no, I think, what's this all about? Has she caught wind of my mum and her dad, I wonder? Or is she going to make a big pass? We go out to the hallway and sit on the stairs.

'Look, Joe,' she says so quietly I almost can't hear,

'I'm not sure this is the right time or place for this, but it's about Merlin. Don't get me wrong, I do really like him, and I don't want to be disloyal, and I know he's your best friend and all that, but . . .'

She hesitates and looks worried.

'But what?' I say. 'Has he being saying nasty things about me?'

'No, nothing like that. It's just a feeling I've got.'

'About what?'

'Look, I could go round and round this for ages.'

'What?'

'Well, you know we've been seeing each other for quite a while now.'

'Yeah. Everyone does.'

'Well, do you ever ask him how it's going?'

'Not really. He always seems as if he doesn't want to talk about it. I know he really likes you, though.'

'Do you want to know how it's going?'

I wonder if this is some sort of a trap, but answer anyway. 'If you want to tell me, sure.'

'Well, the answer is nowhere. It's going nowhere. He seems to have a big problem.'

'Problem? Merlin? What sort of a problem?'

'God, Joe, this is really difficult. He's very affectionate and cuddly and all that, but as soon as it looks as if it might go further – like kissing and stuff – he goes all funny, and seems to want to back off.'

'Perhaps he doesn't fancy you enough,' I say slightly snidely.

38

'Thanks a bunch. You're missing the bloody point.'

'Sorry, Chlo, but I thought Merlin was the randiest thing since Casanova.'

'That's what he likes everyone to think, Joe, but I think there's more to it than all that.'

'Sorry, Chloe, am I being thick? More to what?'

'I think he's got a real problem with girls.'

'The only problem he ever seemed to have was that he couldn't get one.'

'Has it ever occurred to you that he might not really want one?'

'Of course he does. We all do.'

Chloe looks into my eyes, with a sort of pleading look, like I'm not getting what she's trying to say.

'Not all guys do.'

'Course they do. Well, unless they're ga . . .'

I stop in mid sentence and everything seems to go quiet. Chloe holds my hand and speaks very seriously.

'Were you going to say, "unless they're gay", Joe?'

I suddenly feel slightly dizzy. Surely she can't be suggesting that Merlin's . . .

'*Gay?*' I reply, completely shocked. 'Who, Merlin? Are you kidding?'

'No, Joe, I've never been more serious. Worse than that, I don't think he knows it.'

'That's nonsense. Merlin's more hetero than me. I mean, look at the way he's always going on about girls' boobs and bums. Blimey, he was kicked out of Rachel's party last year for stealing her bra.'

'Yeah, and what did he do with it? Lucy told me all about it.'

'Well, he . . . er . . . he did sort of . . . er, well, put it on, I suppose. But that doesn't mean he's gay.'

I suddenly remember reading somewhere that men that go on and on about the size of women's breasts may have a deeply repressed mother fixation. Remembering the way his mum looks in that dress tonight, I'm not surprised.

'And what about all the cross-dressing?' she continues. 'Have you seen what he's got on under that cloak?'

'Not tonight, but I've got a fair idea. Hey, but that's just to shock. That's what Merlin's all about. Anyway, apart from all that, he's crazy about you, and you're not exactly a bloke, are you?'

'Look, Joe, I was sort of crazy about him, and in a way, I still am, but it's him that pulls away when it gets interesting.'

'But he said *you* didn't want anything to do with him physically.'

'He would, wouldn't he? He always says it's my fault when I ask him about it.'

I stare at the ground as my head whirrs like a whirry thing.

'So why are you telling me all this, Chlo?' I ask, almost angrily, 'If it *was* true, what could I do?'

'You're the only person who can help him. The only person he really, really trusts. Look Joe, have you noticed how he's always going on about gays? Taking the piss and that.'

'Yeah, but we all do . . . a bit.'

'But what if Merlin does it because it puts other people off the scent – even him! As long as he takes the mickey out of gays and makes crude jokes about girl's bits, it means he can't be gay himself. Don't you see?'

I feel as if I've been kicked in the stomach. All those evenings we've spent together – laughing, drinking endless cups of tea, talking movies, planning futures. And what about all those times when I was with Lucy, wishing I'd been with Merlin? It couldn't be true. Not my mate Merlin.

'Jeez, Chloe, you don't think I'm gay too . . . do you?' I whisper.

'You, Joe? – are you kidding? I saw the way you were watching me. I'm pretty sure you weren't swatting up on the finer points of modern dance.' That made me go probably more red than I've ever gone before.

'I nearly asked my father to stop the music,' she continues, 'so that someone could put your tongue back in before I tripped over it, Joseph Derby. I tell you what. If you're gay, then I'm the off to lezzie school.' With that, she kisses me ever so softly on the mouth and then disappears.

Blimey O'Reilly, this is another fine mess I'm getting myself into!

My mind is all over the place. I was completely

gobsmacked by what Chloe said, but when I really think about it, I'm not really all that surprised. I suppose something began to occur to me the night I saw him dressed as a witch with stockings and suspenders and all that sparkly stuff. Ever since then there's been this thing at the back of my mind. It's an odd feeling – like an itch you can't scratch. I knew it was something to do with Merlin, but that's as far as it went. It might have had something to do with his being blown away by Chloe's clothes. I'll never really understand dressing up as a girl; the whole idea seems a bit creepy. It's like that Lily Savage bloke. I think he's well-funny and all that, but only when I think of him as a woman. If I let myself imagine that there really is a man under those frocks with a hairy chest and a willie, it all gets a bit gross. I suppose it'd be all right if you were actually gay, but not if you're a regular guy like me or . . . or Merlin.

Having said that, I don't want to sound like a prude. Everyone to their own, I say, as long as it doesn't involve kids or pets or old-age pensioners. But I suppose I knew there was something a bit weird going on with Merlin. I suddenly remember how comfortable Merlin was in that gay bar in Soho on the night of his father's private art show and how horrified he was when the guy who was after him tried to take it further.

What if Chloe is right? What if he really does have a problem with girls? It would certainly explain his lack of scoring. Would he really be happy to be able to talk about it with me? How would I ever be able to face him with it?

If Chloe's right, then I can't just carry on as usual. It throws everything off balance. I mean, what's the point of me going on about all the girls that we know, when he's probably far more interested in the blokes? What would my gran have advised? Knowing her, she'd probably have come straight out with, 'Hello, Merlin dear. Joe tells me that you're a homosexual. How very interesting. Now, would you like a chocolate biscuit or a slice of cherry cake?'

If only it was that easy.

I'm still wrapped up in these thoughts, sitting alone at the back of the garden by the pond when I hear quiet footsteps on the gravel.

Oh no – it's Jade. Even *I'm* not ready for this at the moment.

'Is that you, Joe? Hi babe, what are you doing out here? I've come out for a fag. You look really miserable.'

She sits down. 'Can I help?'

Do I tell her that Chloe thinks her brother could be gay? In a way, she's probably the very best person to talk it over with.

'You know your brother's been seeing Chloe,' I start.

'I wondered if that's what it was about. I saw the look she gave you earlier. Made me quite jealous.'

'No, it's not that. I admit I do quite fancy her, but that's not the problem. Honest. It's something she just said in the house.'

'What, about my brother?'

'Yeah, I don't even know if I can tell you.'

'You've got to now. I won't let you go otherwise.'

In a different situation I would think that was a brilliant idea.

'She said she thinks Merlin's gay . . . Really.'

For once Jade seems lost for words.

'Merlin? But . . . I mean . . . H–how do you make . . . ?' she stammered.

'She thinks that all that talk about boobs and stuff is just a cover-up. She said he seems to have a really hard time when things get even remotely close. She said that she thinks he might really be unhappy underneath, because he hasn't accepted it himself yet.'

'Blimey, Joe, I almost wish I'd never asked what's wrong. It's funny, though. Sky sometimes calls him an old poof and he goes mad. She does it to wind him up.'

'Chloe thinks I'm the person to try to help him. She thinks I should have it out with him.'

'I see her point. Poor old Merlin. I know it can't be true, but if he really is gay, he'll need all the help he can get. You're not homophobic, are you?'

'I don't think so . . . I'm not too wild about it when they come on too heavy, like they did in that bar in Soho, but otherwise I don't give a toss what people get up to.'

'Do you think I should talk about it with my parents?' she asks.

'Maybe you could mention it to your mum. I think your dad might have more of a problem.'

'Oh God,' she murmurs, 'I won't be able to take my

eyes off him now. My poor little broth. Mind you, it might explain why he carries on like he does.'

Back at the party, things are hotting up. Chloe's mum has somehow latched onto my dad, who looks completely out of his depth. Merlin, who's decided to stay wrapped thankfully, is chatting to one of Chloe's ballet school tutors who looks like he doesn't like girls much either. Mum is now avoiding any contact with the wonderful Gerald, who's following her around like the little lost puppy he so obviously is. I get a tap on the shoulder and it's Lucy.

'Where have you been? I just saw Jade coming in from the garden just ahead of you. Are you two getting it together?'

For once I can sound self-righteous with a clear conscience. 'Not at all. We were just talking.'

'That's not what *we* used to do in gardens,' she says, stroking my arm.

'Look Lucy, I . . .'

'Why don't we discuss this in the garden like you just did with Jade?'

'I don't think there's much to talk about . . .'

'Even better, then. All the better for snogging.'

Isn't life funny? You spend ages trying to get a girl back, and then when she hands herself to you on a plate, you feel trapped . . . again! Lucy could have practically any guy she wants, but I'm suddenly the big challenge because I'm resisting. It's all such bollocks. Chloe, on the other hand, doesn't seem to play any games. It's almost like she's a split personality. One side of her is shy and arty and difficult to get through to, but the other is brave and out there and a bit of a show off. There's no doubt about it – if I want to get to know her better, I'll have to find out where Merlin stands in all this. And the sooner the better.

'Joe, I just said something.'

It's Lucy again.

'Aren't you listening?'

'Oh sorry, Lucy, you go outside, I'll just get a drink.'

The wonderful Gerald is by the bar. He turns to me and beams. 'Ah Joe, splendid to see you again. Tell me, have you plans for any more films?'

'Not really. Merlin and I are kicking around a few ideas.'

'What about the one you were telling me about?' I turn around. It's my dad, who's appeared from nowhere.

'Sorry Dad, I can't rememb–'

'You know, the one about the girl who finds out her dad's having an affair with a friend's mother.'

My legs turn to jelly and I look towards the wonderful Gerald, who's gone as white as a sheet.

'I can't quite remember what happened next,' Dad carries on. 'How did it go, Joe? Isn't it the one where they cut him into tiny pieces and feed him to his own dog?'

Dad winks at me, looks across the room at the family's labrador and laughs.

'Black lab, wasn't it?' he adds.

Scene 8

The Kingdom of Joe Derby.
Saturday 11.00 p.m.

ACTION:

After Dad drops his bombshell, I have to get away from the party as soon as possible. I know I'm a wimp, but I just can't stand the embarrassment – or the sight of blood. How the hell had he found out about my mum and the wonderful Gerald? And how had he managed to stay so bloody cool? I also wonder if he'd changed his mind about coming to the concert just so that he could do it there and then. I lie on the bed in my kingdom, wondering what's going to happen – if it hasn't already. After a bit, I hear the front door open downstairs and my mum and dad going quietly to the kitchen. They shut the door behind them – something I've never known them do before.

After an hour or so, I hear a quiet knock on my door.

'Joe, darling, are you awake?'

It's Mum. My mind goes into overdrive. Do I pretend to be asleep, or do I face up to it? Do I pretend I don't know, or do I tell her I've been on the case for a couple of weeks? Shit, Rover, what do I do?

'Do you want to come in, Mum?' I say bravely.

Mum comes in, her eyes red from crying and with long rivulets of mascara down her cheeks.

'I've got something to tell you, Joe darling. I don't really know how to start.'

'I think I know, Mum. You can't keep much of a secret around Northbridge.'

She looked shocked but almost relieved. 'You mean about me and . . .'

'Chloe's dad. 'Fraid so, Ma. Merlin saw you in the Jag.'

'Why didn't you tell me?'

'I reckoned you must have known,' I say, attempting a joke. 'Anyway, what could I say? How you getting on with the guy in the posh car? I don't think so.'

'Are you furious with me, Joe?'

I hadn't really thought about what I thought of her. I knew I wasn't wild about the smug (but wonderful) Gerald, and I knew I'd got a new respect for my old man, but hadn't got much further than that.

'Are you, Joe? I must know.'

'I don't know, Mum. It's really between you and Dad.'

'Does Chloe know anything?'

'I didn't think so, but now you've made me wonder.'

'You didn't say anything?'

'No, Mum, I've got enough problems without all that.'

'It's all such a mess. I've never done anything like this before.'

'How's Dad?' I ask.

'It's incredible. I've never seen him like this before. He doesn't appear to be angry – just hurt. About the nastiest thing he said was, how could I fall for such an awful composer?'

I nearly laugh, but stop just in time.

'I'm afraid I agree, Mum. But I don't suppose music comes into this much.'

'I don't know what to do, Joe. I think I love Gerald, but in a way I love your dad. It's just not the same. We've been together for over twenty years.'

It's odd, but I suddenly see my poor old mum's dilemma. There's Dad, the old model that she's got used to, like a pair of old slippers, and there's the new one – all Jaguars, big hair and posh accents. Anyway, who am I to make a judgement? Look at my situation. I've got three different girls who I can't make my mind up about and a best friend who could be gay.

'You should be a Mormon, Mum. You could have as many husbands as you want, then.'

'Wrong way round. It's only the men that can have as many wives as they want. Typical eh, Joe!'

She looks into my eyes and we almost laugh.

'Has . . . er, Geral . . . Chloe's dad told her mum?' I ask.

'No, he's terrified of her. That's half the problem.'

'Have you asked him to?'

'I haven't had a chance to say anything. We haven't spoken since your dad made that comment about your next film.'

Then she starts crying very quietly. 'I don't want to lose you, Joe. I couldn't bear to be your enemy.'

I sit quietly for a moment looking down at Rover. He seems to have picked up on the mood of the moment and his eyes are glistening. 'What about losing *me*?' he's probably thinking.

'Look, Mum, whatever happens between you and Dad is your business. You're *my* mum, and that's all there is to it.'

Blimey, did I just say that?

She throws her arms round me and kisses the top of my head making it all wet.

'I th–think the best thing is to sleep on it, Joe. I'm going into the spare room. I don't think your father wants me anywhere near him tonight. I'm sorry to have ruined your evening.'

I listen to her go back downstairs and then up to the bathroom. I wait until I hear the spare room door open and close and tiptoe down to the kitchen where I find Dad sitting with a large glass of something that definitely isn't Coca-Cola, staring straight ahead at the fridge door.

He looks up, completely shagged-out looking. He's also been crying.

'Oh hello, Joe. Come on in. Mum tells me that you knew already. Don't you think you should have told me?'

'I would have done, Dad, honest. But not before I'd spoken to Mum. How did you find out?'

'The daft thing is, I didn't really. It only became clear tonight.'

'How come?'

'Well, for a start, I noticed how your mother had changed over the last few weeks. She was more attentive, in a way – always asking me if I was all right and everything. Guilt, I suppose. Then there was all that getting dressed up every night just to go down to the Adult Education Centre.'

'I thought you hadn't noticed.'

'I'm not blind, Joe. One night I checked the community centre. She wasn't there but her car was. I felt terrible tailing my own wife. (Somehow I knew how he felt.)

'How did you know it was Chloe's dad?'

'I didn't – not till tonight. It was the bloody car that did it. I'd seen it leaving the community centre car park just as I was arriving that night. I didn't think any more about it until I saw it again tonight.'

'But you couldn't have been sure.'

'No, but I was as soon as I saw your mum's reaction to my comment about the smooth ride and it costing a lot.'

'How did you know it was his?'

'I'd asked the bloke serving the drinks. I said I was worried because I'd parked a bit close.'

'And then you were sure?'

'Just about. The comment about your next film hammered it home, unfortunately. I thought the smarmy bastard was going to have a heart attack. He shot off like a scalded cat.'

'Dad,' I say admiringly, 'I didn't know you had it in you.'

'There's a lot of things you don't know about me, Joe, and that's my fault. Look, don't get me wrong – I am shocked and really upset. I love your mother and always have, and, I tell you what – I'm not going to give her up

51

without a fight, especially to an arse-hole like him.'

I've never heard my old man talking like that, and I'm not sure I like it. But then I think, I've problems of my own due to all this. What do I do about Chloe, for a start? I hardly think it bodes well for us getting anything together. Imagine if we ever got married, with *my* dad punching *her* dad's lights out (that's after Merlin punches mine out). Jeez, it sounds even worse than my sister Zoe's wedding. I then think about Zoe! What's she going to say about all this? And Mr Smug from Smugsville, my sister's husband Graham?

Just as I'm going up to bed the phone rings. It's gone twelve but I'm fairly sure I know who it is and grab it on its second ring.

'Hello Joe, I'm sorry to call you so late.'

'Hi, is that you Chloe? Are you all right?' I can tell she's been crying from the slight catch in her voice.

'I just had to get away from the noise downstairs. My parents sound as if they're going to tear each other's head off. I think my dad's been seeing another woman.'

Don't I know it.

'I sort of know, Chloe. Look, I'm really sorry.'

'How do you know? I didn't think you knew my father.'

'I don't, but I know my mother.'

'Sorry, Joe, I don't know what you're talking about. What's your mother got to do with it?'

Breathe deeply, Joey boy. 'I'm afraid she's the other woman.'

'What do you mean? Your mum and my dad?'

'I'm afraid so, I've known for a couple of weeks. I saw them in a car park. Before you go on at me, I've just had my own dad having a go at me for not telling him.'

'I don't believe this. My dad's been having an affair with your mum.'

Chloe's silent for almost a minute.

'Are you all right?' I ask.

'Er, yeah, I think so. It's all a bit of a shock. What do you make of it?'

'God knows. It's beginning to sound like both of our parents' marriages were accidents waiting to happen.'

'Christ, Joe, we must be almost related by all this, but I can't think what we'd be called.'

'Broken homers-in-law, I suppose.'

I hear a stifled giggle at the other end.

'What a terrible night for you, Joe. First you're told your best mate's a poof and then that you and I are soon to be in the same family.'

'I can think of worse people to be related to, Chloe.'

'Does that mean we can't have children?'

Shit, did she really say that? It's my turn to laugh, but out loud this time. 'Blimey, Chloe, even *I'm* thinking of turning gay after all this.'

'Don't do it too soon, Joe. We need to go out first.'

As I slowly drag myself up the wooden hill to beddy-byes, I wonder what the world's all about.

Scene 9

The Labardia house.
Tuesday 8.30 a.m.

ACTION:

When I call in at Merlin's house on the way to school, I find him leaping around like a mad thing.

'Joe, you'll never guess what's happened.'

'Hopefully we're off to mind-reading school,' I say, maybe a little too sarcastically.

'We've just had a letter from *Whatzit* – you know, that kids' telly programme on Saturday mornings.'

'Blimey,' I say. 'How did they know about us?'

'Apparently that guy who interviewed us from the local newspaper knew the producer or something. He must have remembered my address.'

'What do they want?'

'They want us to go on the show to talk about *La Maison Doom*. They might even play a bit on telly.'

I'm stood there staring at him, open mouthed and lost for words.

'Are you winding me up? Let's have a look.'

Merlin hands me the letter.

Dear Mr Labardia and Mr Derby,

An old colleague of mine from your local paper, the Northbridge Gazette, *told me that you have written and produced a short film that has been extremely well received. We think we might be able to talk about it on Whatzit. Would you be able to come in to our studios and be interviewed by Kenny Dixon and Emma Palethorpe. If you like the idea, could you ring me at the number below and we could discuss details. In the meantime , perhaps we could send a courier to pick up a copy of your film and maybe a brief biography of yourselves. Your fees will be discussed in due course.*

Yours sincerely,
Penelope Jones
Executive Producer

'What am I going to wear?' is all I can think of saying.

Merlin laughs. 'This is the break we've been waiting for, Joey boy. I'll think I'll pack up school today.'

'And do what?' I say

'Be a film director. Blimey, Joe, we're halfway there.'

'What would we live on?' I ask, boringly.

'Well, we could live at home until we're famous.'

'Oh yeah,' I say, 'I can just see me telling my mum and dad that I'll be living at home for nothing until I'm famous. I think they might have a few problems of their own without that.'

'What's happening with all that? Is your mum hitting the road?'

'Search me. It's bloody awful in our house. Everyone's pretending nothing's happened. Even Rover.'

'Is she still seeing what's-his-face?'

'I don't think so. I don't think Chloe's old lady'll let the prat out of her sight.'

'She's dead scary. I wouldn't want to get her excited.'

'My mum's just got a mobile, so I suppose she and the wonderful Gerald can text each other.'

'Safe text, I think they call that.'

I ignore the attempt at a joke.

'How's your dad?' he continues

'It's weird, he's sort of changed. Instead of trying to be all sort of nice to her, he's started bossing her around. Treat 'em mean, keep 'em keen sort of thing. The daft thing is, she seems to be going along with it.'

'Maybe that's the sort of bloke she wanted all along. Unless it's guilt that's stopping her from going ballistic.'

'Chloe seems to quite like the idea of her mum and dad splitting up.'

'I reckon that's because she'll get more chance to speak to you.'

'What?'

'C'mon, Joe, I'm not daft . . . or blind. I've seen the way you two get on.'

'But, I . . .'

'Look, man, I don't mind. I've decided I don't really fancy her. Too skinny for me. I'm into big women.'

'Is that right?' I say, trying not to sound miffed.

'What d'you mean? You know I am.'

'You always say you are, but you never seem to get hold of any.'

'Yeah, well, I'm too busy. They can wait.'

I hesitate for a second. This is as good a time as any to take the plunge, I reckon. 'Any other reasons?'

Merlin stops in his tracks and stares at me. He has a strange defensive look in his eye.

'What are you getting at, Joe? What other bloody reasons *could* there be?'

'Oh, I don't know. Maybe you don't really like girls at all. Stranger things have happened.'

'Are you saying . . . ?'

'I'm not saying anything Merlin. It just seems that the sort of stuff you get up to with girls isn't very . . .'

'Are you saying you think I'm gay?'

'I'm just suggesting that maybe you . . .'

'Well, you can just f . . . k off.'

With that, he crosses the road and stalks off to school double-quick, as if I've just stuck a lighted rocket up his arse.

Well, Joey boy, you couldn't have handled that much worse.

My house.
6.00 p.m.

All through school, Merlin avoided me like the plague. Everyone noticed, as we're usually inseparable, but no one dared ask why. I feel completely miserable. Christ, I've just called my best mate a homo.

I ring Chloe's mobile.

'Hi Joe, how you doing? Do you want me to ring you back on the land-line?'

She rings back. 'Are you OK? You sound a bit low.'

'I'm all right . . . sort of. I had The Conversation with Merlin this morning.'

'*Reeeee*ally! Was it about you-know-what? Flipping hell, Joe, how did it go?'

'He went through the roof. Told me to f-off. I haven't spoken to him all day. I just feel terrible. I hope he's all right.'

'Would you like me to ring him? I won't say anything about what you said. If there's anything to report, I'll come straight back to you.'

I put the phone down and go upstairs to lie on my bed. I must be mad, suggesting my best mate's gay. About half an hour later the phone rings and Mum says it's for me.

It's Chloe.

'Hi Joe, it's me. I've just spoken to Merlin.'

'Is he still going ape-shit?'

'No, if anything he was a bit quiet. He said he had a lot of thinking to do.'

'Really? About whether I'm a bastard or not?'

'He said he doesn't know what he thinks at the moment. Look, Joe, this isn't about you, it's about poor Merlin.'

'Sorry, Chloe,' I say.

'He said he could hardly believe his ears when you said what you said to him.'

'Does he still want to be my friend?'

'Probably more so, Joe. He says he feels very alone at the moment. I think you should just give him a ring and say something about liking him whatever he is . . . I don't know. I said I was going to ring you.'

'I'm not sure I know what to say. It's not every day your best mate goes over to the other side.'

'I think if he can make *you* understand how he feels about stuff, it might help. If you want my opinion, I think you could be more help than anyone else on earth.'

I ring Merlin and say basically what Chloe had suggested. He thanks me, but when I suggest going over there, he tells me he needs some time to sort himself out. Then he asks if I could not mention this to anyone else.

Scene 10

Merlin's dungeon.
Friday 7.30 p.m.

ACTION:

It's been a dead tricky week. Merlin and I have been fine, but this whole gay thing's been hanging over us like a big black, or should I say pink, cloud. He knows that I'm thinking about it and I know that he is. It's Friday evening and he rings me and asks if I want to go round. At last, with a bit of luck it might come out into the open, one way or the other.

Merlin's sitting alone in his room, drinking a beer and playing the soundtrack from *Cabaret*. It's one of the few musicals he likes – I don't like *any*, except perhaps the *Rocky Horror Picture Show*!

At first, we just sit looking at each other, neither knowing where to start. But then I decide to jump in feet first.

'Look, mate, I'm sorry I said what I did, when I did. It just came out. I've felt like a real cretin all week.'

'Don't worry, Joe. In a way I'm rather grateful. I knew there was something wrong – sorry, not *wrong* – a bit odd, but I just couldn't put my finger on it. You brought it out into the open, that's all. That's what best mates are for, isn't it?'

'I'm not sure best mates accuse each other of being gay,' I said.

'The thing is, until you mentioned it, it hadn't really occurred to me that I might be. This week's been dead weird, I've just been going round and round in circles.'

'Where did you land?'

Merlin takes a large swig of lager and smiles.

'I'm afraid, dear boy, you were more or less bang on. The penny hadn't dropped that's all. Life's been pretty bloody awful lately. I haven't even been able to say the word *gay*. How did you guess, anyway?'

'It was just something Chloe said. It suddenly sort of made sense.'

'Was it about it being my fault that her and I never seem to get anywhere?'

'Yeah, sort of.'

He smiles again, almost like he's relieved.

'It's not that I don't like girls, like you suggested. I just don't really fancy them.'

'What, none of them?'

'Not really. I can see if they're beautiful and all that. Going out with Chloe was like being given a really fab car, but not being able to drive it. You see, I don't hate women ... if anything, I want to be *like* them, rather than *into* them – if you know what I mean.'

Merlin giggles at his own bad joke.

'What about blokes? Do you fancy *them*?'

'I know this must sound dead weird, but I think I probably do. Especially if they're slightly camp and funny.'

'Like who?'

'Oh, you know, guys like Julian Clary and Eddie Izzard.'

'Would you like to – er – sort of kiss them and all that?'

'Yeah, why not?'

'And more than that?'

Merlin laughs and puts his arm round my shoulder.

'Look, don't worry, Joe. You're safe with me. I don't think there's a lot of doubt about where you're coming from.'

'So what *are* you going to do?'

'Don't really know. I told my mum and she was bloody brilliant. She said that her and Dad had been wondering for a while, but had just waited for me to come to them. It's funny, I've always known my Uncle Julian, her brother, was gay and Mum says she remembered that he'd been like that since they were young, so she got used to it.'

'What about Jade and Sky?'

'I asked Mum to tell them. They were really cool, apparently. They even said I could borrow their clothes, but I think that was a joke.'

'Do you really like being a girl – sorry – being dressed as a girl?'

'It's not what you think, Joe. I'm not doing it to pull blokes – well I don't think so. I just like being able to use make-up and wear over-the-top clothes. I've always thought women were dead lucky. They can choose whether to look sexy or not whenever they feel like it. We blokes are always expected to be the same, more or less.'

'How are you going to handle school? Do you want to keep it a secret?'

'It's funny, there's a couple of guys who I reckon know already. It takes one to know one, sort of thing. Anyway, I'm not going to deny it. No one would dare take the piss out of me.'

He's certainly right there. Merlin's quicker than anyone I've ever met when it comes to the old banter, and quite aggressive with it.

'It could be quite a laugh being the school gay,' he continues. 'You know me, I can handle all the attention I can get.'

'What about Chloe?'

'No need to say anything, really. You were right, Joe – she must be pretty sure already. A couple of times she really got arsy with me, when I wouldn't play. It was quite strange, really. At first she wouldn't have anything to do with me, despite all my suggestive comments. It was just a game girls play, though. After a bit she was dying to get down to it and then I wouldn't play.'

'Do you think she'll still like you?' I ask.

'In a funny way, I don't think it will matter that much. I think she's going to turn out to be as close a mate as you are.'

'How would you feel if I went out with her?'

'As long as you don't go all soppy and cut me out, I don't give a toss. You know what you were like with Lucy.'

'Yeah, but it didn't last long, did it?'

'Shit man, if I was you, I'd worry more about what Lucy'll do if she finds out. She'll have you altered surgically, and I dread to think where.'

My mind wanders for a few seconds. 'I can't believe I didn't spot it sooner,' I say.

'What?'

'That you were . . . er . . . gay.'

'You're not kidding. I'm amazed I didn't spot it sooner either.'

'You really didn't know?'

'I knew things weren't sort of normal, but then there's nothing normal in my family, anyway.'

I start laughing. 'I don't think your sisters are gay,' I say.

'It's beginning to sound pretty good, being gay and stuff. Anyway, I can always change my mind later.'

'Jeez, Merlin, you can't be gay just when you feel like it.'

'Why not? Some people fiddle around in both camps for years. Look at David Bowie – and he ended up with a real babe.'

'That doesn't seem fair to me.'

'It's brilliant. You can pick and choose, like what colour you have your hair.'

'What? Like, I think I'll be gay today?'

'Yeah, why not? I think that's the way I'll play it at school. That way no one can feel safe from my irresistible charms.'

'I'm sure some of us can,' I laugh.

Scene 11

The television studios.
Saturday 10.00 a.m.

ACTION:

Only Merlin could have gone through what he has this past week and come out of it OK. He seems to have snapped back to the way he was ages ago – as if a weight's been lifted off his shoulders. It's Saturday morning and we're sitting in the reception at the television studios waiting to meet this Penelope woman, – the producer of *Whatzit*. I was dreading what Merlin was going to turn up in, but, thank God, he's toned down his image and looks almost restrained in a shiny blue suit and a shirt and tie. He's even had his hair cut a bit. He still has dreads, of course, but shorter ones. Merlin must really want this gig.

'Are you nervous?' I ask.

'Nah, not really. I can't wait. I just hope it's not going to be too kidsy.'

'I'm dead scared, mate. Maybe you should have done this on your own.'

'Don't worry about it. You'll be fine. Just follow me.'

A girl with a clipboard and a cut-off T-shirt that says 'Bitch', comes through the far door and walks straight up to us.

'Are you Merlin and Joe? I'm Janey, the researcher. I've come to collect you.'

'You can collect me any time,' whispers Merlin under his breath, forgetting his new status.

Janey's about twenty-something and a real top-draw, no-questions-asked, babe, guaranteed to make me even more nervous than I am already.

Merlin finds his proper voice. 'Hi, I'm Merlin. This is Joe, my partner.'

I've never been called a partner before and, to tell the truth, I rather like it, despite it's slightly dodgy overtones.

'Would you like to come and meet Penny? She's our producer. She'll fill you in on what's going to happen. I think they've scheduled you in fairly early, so there won't be too much hanging around.'

'Cool . . . we're fairly used to studios,' says Merlin (Crown Prince of Bullshitters).

Penny Jones turns out to be a loudish, fattish woman, wearing an appalling sort of rainbow-coloured kaftan and bright red glasses on a bright red chain. She speaks so fast it's as if she's just heard there's going to be a world ban on talking.

'Oh there you are, darling hearts. How simply wonderful of you to come. Let me introduce you to Kenny and Emms before they go on air.'

I've only seen *Whatzit* a couple of times before and hated it. Most of all I hated the boy presenter called Kenny, who speaks with a real put-on, Nigel Kennedy-type Cockney accent and has a face like a nursery for spots (even under the make-up).

'Hiya,' he shouts, 'Whadda you two do? You a boy band or somefing?'

Merlin turns round and gives him a classic Clint Eastwood narrow-eyed stare.

'No, we're a thirty-piece symphony orchestra,' he says, omitting the customary 'dickhead' bit.

Emma, who's slightly posh and all off-centre pony-tail, pierced belly-button and glittery chest, looks at us like we're something she's just scraped off her shoe.'

'I think these are the kids that made the film thingy. Is that right, Pen?'

'That's right, honeybunch. I never managed to see it – you know what it's like – but it sounds ever such fun, darling.'

Oh *merde*! This really is not going well. Merlin's beginning to look decidedly miffed. Nobody calls him a kid and gets away with it, and as for not even bothering to see our film . . .

'What's it about?' Emma asks.

'What's what about?' he says stroppily

'Your marvellous film.'

'Stuffing!' says Merlin. 'Serial stuffing.'

Kenny, who can only think of the sexual meaning of stuffing, looks gobsmacked and starts to giggle.

I jump in to try and save the day.

'It's about two Parisian taxidermists' daughters who murder and stuff their dad for ruining their mother's life. Then they do the same to all the policemen who come round to see what's going on.'

'Charming! Is there anyone famous in it?' says Emma, already beginning to look bored.

'It all depends what you call famous,' says Merlin snottily. 'There aren't any boy bands or soap stars if that's what you're after. But there is a famous artist in it. My father actually.'

Fat Penny jumps in like a referee at a boxing match.

'Well, that's all lovely, then. I see you're all going to get along brilliantly. Anyway, I've just had the nod from upstairs. We're about to start the show. If you and Joe want to watch how we do it, you can sit over there behind the cameras.'

I've been studying kids' TV programmes since I was a kid, and if you ever look either side of the manic presenters, you can see that most of the kids in the audience look bored out of their wits . . . picking their noses, fiddling with their name badges, looking anywhere but where they're supposed to and no doubt wishing they were on the mini-bus home with a chocolate milkshake and a Big Mac. Every now and again the production crew round them up like gormless sheep and force them to clap and yell out mindless crap to make it look like they're having a good time. It doesn't fool me.

This lot are no exception, being forced to sit around while Kenny and Emma make total prats of themselves, shouting at each other like there's a ten-foot-thick brick wall between them.

There's a break for a cartoon and then plumpster Penny waddles over to where me and Merlin are sitting.

'Right-o, luvvies, you're on next. Would you like to go over to Kenny and Emms?'

Kenny and Emma are sitting in the middle of a set resembling Hamley's after a terrorist attack, with too goofy-looking puppets that might have been cut out of a shag-pile lavatory rug. You can even see their operators' feet under the table.

I feel so nervous I could wet myself.

Kenny kicks off.

'Now kids, let have a real *Whatzit* welcome for two real-live Steven Spielbergs, Mervyn Labardia and Joe Derby.'

'MERLIN!' shouts Merlin over the kids, who've been goaded into grudging enthusiasm.

'What?' Kenny shouts back.

'You called me Mervyn. My name's Merlin, you . . .'

Kenny looks all confused, having been knocked off his script. Emma takes over.

'These two cool guys have made a brilliant film called *La Maison Doom*, which, as all you brainiac French speakers know, means *The House of Doom*.'

The two puppets, now wearing berets, bounce around pretending to be French.

'How do you know?' says Merlin, knocking the beret off the puppet who's started to tweak his dreadlocks.

'Know what?' says Emma, trying not to appear annoyed.

'How do you know it's a brilliant film?' continues Merlin. 'None of you lot have even bothered to watch it.'

'What made you decide to be film directors?' Kenny breaks in, veering away from the subject like a drunk driver.

'Nothing *made* us do bloody anything, we just felt like it,' groans Merlin.

The kids on either side start giggling. It's funny, at first I was really embarrassed, but suddenly I realise I'm beginning to get into this. Even my nervousness is beginning to fade.

'Well, it all sounds fantabuloso to me,' shouts Emma. 'Anyway, we mustn't hold you up, I expect you two will be jetting off to Hollywood after this.'

It's my turn. 'Why?'

Now she really does start showing signs of losing the plot. 'Because that's where all the most famous movie directors end up, isn't it?'

'It could well be,' I say, 'but we're just students from Northbridge High, who happen to have made a film. Why don't you stop talking such pants?'

I can't believe I just said that.

Kenny bursts in, trying to keep the whole thing sweet.

'Just think of all those young beautiful babes queuing up for parts in your films.'

'No use to me,' laughs Merlin,

'Why's that?'

'I'm gay, that's why,' announces Merlin triumphantly.

Total silence from Kenny and Emma. Even the crew look shocked. I can hardly believe he said that and nor can anyone else. Who but Merlin would 'come out' on national television?

At this point, one of the stupid puppets starts fiddling with my tie. As if to break the silence, I lash out as hard as I can and send the damn thing's head spinning across the studio, leaving a naked hand sticking out of its furry shoulders and not quite knowing what to do. This seems to be the signal for the director to yell 'CUT!', but no one hears him. Kenny, feeling totally humiliated, tries to push Merlin, who, dodging like a prize-fighter, forces him to fall across the two puppeteers. Seconds later, there appears to be scrum of telly people and decapitated puppets milling around on the floor, with fat Penny screaming as if a rat's just run up her drawers. A couple of kids on either side, thinking this is all part of the show, come piling in and start pummelling presenter and puppet alike.

Merlin's laughing, fit to burst. I catch his eye and make a sign for the exit.

As we tear out of the front entrance and hit the street, we both realise our television careers might have to go on hold for the present.

'I wonder how much of that actually went out,' Merlin giggles.

'I expect we just might find out fairly soon. We told everyone we know to watch.'

* * *

Back at Merlin's the phone hardly stops ringing. Just about all of our mates caught the action. Apparently, because the telly people only had a few seconds of safety time, they only managed to cut to the ads just as the kids piled in. After the break, a visibly shaken Kenny and Emma tried to make out it was all a great big spoof and that we'd all been in on it. Spoof my arse. No one who knows us is fooled a bit. Best of all, no one mentions Merlin saying he was gay. They obviously all thought it was a great joke.

'That suits me fine,' he says. 'By the time everyone realises I wasn't joking, they'll have forgotten all about it. I can now say I'm gay all the time and everyone can choose to believe what they want. It couldn't be better, man.'

Scene 12

The Labardia house.
Sunday 9.30 a.m.

ACTION:

It's Sunday morning and all hell's broken loose. Apart from my mum and dad being more than usually grumpy (saying I showed them up and all that), everyone's been ringing us, trying to find out what happened after Merlin and I got shut down.

When I get round to Merlin's, I find out it's not as bad as I thought. Someone from the TV company rang him earlier to let us know our brief appearance yesterday caused a bit of a riot. Kids from all over have been ringing in saying how brilliant they thought it was and asking when can they see us again. US AGAIN! More to the point, they all want to see *La Maison Doom*. Apparently the TV company are now in a real funk because, when they finally got round to watching it, they realised that it wasn't suitable for little kids. Poxy Penny might be fired for not doing her job properly – ha ha!

'How do you know all this?' I ask when he's stopped laughing.

'Do you remember Janey – you know, the babe that came to meet us in reception? It was her that rang. She also said that practically all the kids really hated those prats Kenny and Emma anyway, and the TV company's been swamped with phone calls and text messages

73

congratulating us for making them look so bloody stupid.'

Merlin's phone rings.

'Hello . . . yes, this is Merlin Labardia . . . Sorry, who did you say? . . . Oh, er, right.' There's a long pause while Merlin listens intently to the person on the other end. Then he speaks in a slightly shakey voice. 'Are you serious? . . . This isn't a wind-up, is it? . . . Yeah, you bet. We'd love to . . . a week Saturday, did you say? . . . You'll let me know where and when . . . yeah, OK . . . bye.'

'Who was it this time?' I ask.

Merlin, who's pretty pale anyway, seems to have gone a shade paler and is hardly able to speak. 'It was the boss of the TV company that makes *Whatzit*. She said she couldn't go into it in detail now, but she says they've been rethinking their children's programming for some time. They're looking for something completely new. She asked if we'd like to meet the executives next weekend.'

'Us? Why?'

'Why d'you think, dumbo?'

'They don't want us to . . . ?'

Merlin cuts me off. 'They want us to come to their office next Saturday to talk and maybe do some tests. They've been working on a kids' arts programme.'

'What do you mean?'

'Blimey, Joe, you know . . . books, movies, young artists, new bands, dancers – all that sort of stuff. I think they're interested in having us present it. We'd be a kind of arty Ant and Dec, but not so naff.'

'Shit man, I can't do that,' I say.

Merlin looks puzzled.

'Why not?'

'I'd just be too self-conscious.'

'You didn't seem that bad yesterday.'

'That's because they were such prats. It didn't matter.'

'But we'd do it differently,' he says. 'They don't want any of that corny leaping about and shouting bollocks any more, or so she said. We could just be ourselves.'

I go quiet for a few seconds.

'Look, mate, I never really wanted to be out front,' I eventually say. 'That's why I never did drama or anything at school. Honest, Merlin, I might have to think about this.'

A look of frustration crosses his face. 'Well, don't ruin it for me,' he says. 'They might not just want *one* of us.'

My house.
11.45 a.m.

When I get home, Mum and Dad are waiting for me. I want to tell them what's just happened, but now obviously isn't the time. I can always tell when something's up. And I don't know what it is about but there's a grey cloud of doom hanging over the place.

'Joe darling,' says Mum. 'Could you come into the kitchen? Your father and I have something to tell you.'

'Oh no, you're not still going on about that TV business?' I say.

They both laugh nervously.

'No dear, it's nothing to do with that,' says Mum. 'It's about us – me and your father. We've decided it might be better if I moved out. You know things haven't being going too well between us, don't you?'

'Where are you going to live?' I ask.

'With a friend from work for a while, until we see how things turn out.'

'When are you going?'

'As soon as possible. Probably this evening. Look, I'm sorry, Joe darling, but it's for the best. We can't carry on pretending nothing's happened.'

Back in my kingdom I lie on the bed with Rover, trying to make sense of everything that's going on. Bloody brilliant, isn't it? Just as I'm getting my head round the idea that I might be a TV star, I find out I'm soon to be the product of a broken home. Christ, I'm a statistic.

It's funny, I don't feel exactly broken-hearted, but I do feel *something*, and whatever it is ain't good. I just can't imagine the house without my mum around. And poor old Dad . . . what the hell's *he* going to do? He can't wash, or iron, or cook, or bloody anything.

Talking about cooking . . . Forget Dad – what am I going to do? Jeez, I might have to go round to Mum's every night to get some decent grub.

I start wondering what's going on over at Chloe's. I wonder if her father's moving out too. Probably not. I wouldn't mind betting my mum's going to end up holding the crappy end of the stick.

I suddenly *have* to speak to Chloe. Mum and Dad are still in the kitchen and I can just about make out from the low drone of their voices that they're trying to talk quietly without me hearing. Suits me. Two can play at that game. I tiptoe down the stairs, dial Chloe's mobile and then go as far back up the stairs as the phone lead will let me.

'Hello.'

'Hi Chloe, it's Joe,' I say quietly. 'Can you talk?'

'Hi sweet. How you doing? Yeah, Mum and Dad are out. Tell you what – ring us back on the ordinary phone. It'll be cheaper.'

I go back downstairs, write down the number on the pad next to the phone, then slip back up and dial again.

'You sounded worried, Joe. What's going on? Nothing to do with being on TV, was it? It's such a drag, I didn't see it. I had to be at school for a stupid tap class – it's part of the course. Everyone says you and Merlin were brilliant. They're all talking about it. Don't worry, just about everyone I know's videoed it. I can't miss your moment of fame, can I?'

'Actually it's about our parents. Your dad and my mum.'

'Oh that. What's happened now?'

'My mum's leaving my dad, that's what. Probably tonight.'

'Oh Joe, that's terrible. It should never have come to that. Not because of my stupid dad. Where's she going?'

'I'm not sure. She says she's going to stay with a friend. Do you know if she's still seeing your dad?'

'I doubt it. He and mum have gone to the marriage guidance place tonight. What a bloody joke. Talk about closing the stable door after the horse has bolted. This isn't the first time this has happened. I know of at least three other poor misguided women he's fiddled around with.'

'How come? How does he get away with it?'

'He doesn't! My mother usually gives him a damn good hiding and he gets back into his basket – it's as simple as that. She's become *his* mum, you see. He couldn't do anything without her. That's why he always jumps back into line. It's so bloody pathetic.'

'What a prat! – oops, sorry.'

'Don't worry, I understand how you're feeling. I even had a go at him the other night. Honest, Joe, the atmosphere's the real pits in our house. The thing is, Mum's really had enough this time. I think she gave him a big ultimatum the other night. Behave yourself or piss off sort of thing!'

'I'm more worried about *my* mum,' I say. 'She must be feeling bloody awful. Not only is her life ruined, my dad's is too.'

'Poor old Joe. I wish I could say sorry on his behalf.'

'Don't be daft, Chlo. We can't help having the parents we have. Christ, sometimes I wish I could say I was found on the doorstep.'

'I'm terrified of turning out like either of mine,' Chloe

says quietly. 'Sometimes I catch myself saying things that sound just like my flipping mother. She's so bossy she makes even my general studies teacher seem like a pussy cat.'

'Are you bossy?'

'I can be. I was terrible with Merlin. That's why it's good that it all came to nothing. It's only certain sorts of people that bring it out and he's one of them, poor bloke. I suppose it's the same with my mum. Oh hell, I hadn't thought of that.'

'At least you've warned me,' I say.

(There are certain times when I say things that I would give just about anything to take back. That was one of them.)

'Warned you about what, Joe?' says Chloe, in a dead sexy voice. 'Have you got plans regarding me, then?'

Oh blimey, here we go. Let's see if old smarty-pants Joe Derby can get himself out of this one.

'Er, no – I mean, I haven't really thought . . . well, I have thought . . . but not, um, that's to say . . . I, er – oh, shit . . .'

Chloe's laughter is practically deafening.

'It's all right, Joe, don't get your knickers in a twist. If it's going to happen, it will. I didn't know whether you even fancied me until the other night.'

I go bright red, but thankfully no one can see.

'Yeah, well, I do, sort of. Well, not just sort of . . . I mean – er – well, I think I . . .'

Chloe is giggling.

'I should shut up,' she says, 'or you'll end up never talking to me again. Anyway, there's Lucy still hanging around. She's never been someone to take no for an answer.'

'Do you still see as much of her?' I ask.

'I try not too. She's bit of an air-head. All she thinks about is clothes and boys. She's all right to go out with occasionally and you always get a lot of good-looking guys hanging round. You've met her mum and dad haven't you?'

'You bet. I call them the Upwardly-Mobiles.'

'You won't believe it – my dad even had a go at her mum at one of their ghastly barbecues.'

'You're joking. He doesn't hang around. What did she do?'

'Very little, luckily. She's only into toy-boys, or so Lucy tells me. I heard she even hit on you a bit.'

'*Even* me,' I answer, trying to sound hurt.

'Sorry, but you know what I mean. Apparently she made a real pass at that Sixth-Form guy that went out with Lucy after you.'

'Who, James Burton? You're joking. He's such a prat. What did he do?'

'He really went for it, apparently. That's what split him and Lucy up. Her mum denied everything, of course, but Lucy knows something went on in their summer house.'

'Do you think they actually did it?'

'Who knows? I wouldn't put anything past her.'

'What did her old man say?'

'Him? He wouldn't have spotted anything going on if he was in there *with* them. He only cares about his cars and his garden.'

'It all goes on in Northbridge,' I say. 'Jeez, I'm going to look at my mates' mums and dads more closely from now on.'

'Listen, Joe, I know this isn't how it's supposed to be done, but can we go out some time – as mates? I've talked to Merlin about it and he's cool. Especially now that he's out of the closet.'

'What do you think about all that?' I ask.

'I think it's great. I really love Merlin, honest, but not in that way. Anyway, you didn't answer my question.'

'Sorry, Chloe. Yeah, I think that would be really good. I need another good friend at the moment.'

'But lets not go *too* far down the "just good friends" road,' she says with a giggle.

Whatever turns out to be wrong with Chloe (there's bound to be something), it won't be her sense of humour, that's for sure.

Scene 13

Northbridge High School.
Thursday 9.35 a.m.

ACTION:

Ever since Mum left on Sunday night, a deathly hush has come over the house. It's as if some gremlin's sucked away all its spirit . . . It doesn't even seem like a home anymore – just a place where Dad and I (and Rover and Tweetie) happen to eat and sleep. The poor old bloke's bustling around trying to look busy, but I can tell he's really hurting inside. Even Rover's hanging about by the back door whining in a kind of doggy daze. I wonder how Mum's doing?

I decide I just *have* to see my mum and let her know that whatever she's done and whatever else happens, I'm still her son and her mate. She must be feeling terrible now.

At break-time I ring the shop on Merlin's mobile. It's her lunch break and she answers.

'Hi Mum, it's Joe. Remember me?'

'Joe darling, how lovely. How are you? How are things at home?'

She sounds as if she's on the verge of tears.

'Well, you only left the other day, but everything seems dead weird without you, Mum. Are you all right?'

'It was ever so strange sleeping in someone else's place, but Cathy's been wonderful.'

'Can I see you soon? I've told Dad I'm ringing you and he's cool. I think he's missing you too.'

'I know, Joe. It must all seem a bit strange, but I've got loads of stuff to sort out, and I couldn't do it there. Whatever happens, life's going to be different from now on.'

I take the bull by the horns and ask the big question. 'What about the other bloke, Ma?'

'The least said about him the better. Thank God I saw the light when I did.'

'Does that mean you'll be coming home soon?'

'I know this sounds funny, darling, but all this has really nothing to do with Gerald. He was just a symptom, not a cause. It really could have been anyone. The problem was really between me and your dad. We'd worked ourselves into a corner, you see, and I just couldn't go on living like that. That's why I got into the stupid affair in the first place. I don't even really like Gerald that much. He's such a big girl's blouse.'

I've never heard my mum talk like this.

'Will you see Dad again?'

'Of course, Joe. I have to come back at the weekend to get more stuff. Listen, I don't hate him. Come to that, now I've got some space to think about it, I don't even really dislike him. It's just that we'd both stopped trying and that's like a living death.'

'When can I see you, Mum?'

'Any time you like. Why don't you meet me after work tomorrow? We could go for a drink.'

Blimey, I never thought I'd be meeting my own mum in a pub. This could be quite a laugh.

Although it's only a few days since Merlin announced to the world that he was gay, the reaction at school has been almost the opposite of what I'd expected. Instead of being picked on or having the mickey taken, it seems as if most of our peers think it's quite cool – even the yobs in Year Ten, who think you're a poof if you don't like football. Peculiar.

Merlin's gone and told all the kids at school about our meeting at the television studios and they're all giving us the third degree. 'How much dosh are you going to make?' 'Can we come to the recording?' 'Do you reckon you'll get to meet Kat Deeley?'

One kid from Year Nine came up to Merlin this morning and asked for his autograph. It's dead weird, but for a moment I was really pissed off because she didn't ask for mine.

Worse still, I told a few friends earlier that I wasn't all that keen on being a presenter, and that it was more Merlin's thing than mine, but now Spike Davis is practically begging Merlin to go in my place, and I feel all funny and even a bit arsy. Maybe I'm more into the fame thing than I thought.

'Listen, mate, who made the bloody film? You didn't,' I say.

Merlin stares at me incredulously.

'But you said you didn't want to do it,' says Spike.

'That doesn't mean I want *you* to,' I reply, feeling like the kid at Christmas who's fed up with a particular toy but doesn't want anyone else to play with it.

'That's pathetic,' says Spike, looking like he's going to clock me one.

'Well, you go out and make a bloody film, then,' I say, squaring up for a bit of pushing and shoving.

But suddenly we both see the funny side of it and piss ourselves laughing instead.

My house.
4.30 p.m.

As I'm approaching my house, I see my brother-in-law Graham's soppy Japanese sports car parked in front. No doubt the jungle drums have reached Meldrew Close or wherever they bloody live.

My sister Zoe and her ever-expanding husband must have taken time off work to come over. They've let themselves in and are waiting in the front room. Poor old Dad's still at work, thank God, so he won't have to put up with this on top of everything else.

I know it sounds a bit mean, but anyone who knows me well knows just how much I can't stand my big sister. Mind you, if finding a parter who matches your personality is an art, then Zoe must have been inspired when choosing Graham. He's the most pompous, self-important prat I've ever met.

Zoe, who's only been married six months or so, is

either getting fat in sympathy with her husband or is showing the first signs that Graham really does have some lead in his pencil after all.

'So is it true?' she demands angrily, flying into instant attack mode.

'Is *what* true?' I reply with mock puzzlement.

'You know what I'm talking about. This thing with Mum.'

'You mean her *affair*?' I say, making her wince visibly. This could turn out to be fun after all.

'Yes, if you like. How long have you known about it?'

'Oh I don't know, maybe a few weeks.'

'Why didn't you tell us?'

'You didn't ask. And anyway, I really didn't think you'd particularly want to know that your mum's having it off with someone else.' I must admit I *am* beginning to enjoy this.

'You're disgusting. It's absolutely awful. I suppose we're going to have to sort it out?'

'If it's a problem for you, don't come round.'

'Why are you being like this? . . . I feel terrible. . . my own mother!' She begins to snivel and Graham puts his arm around her and glowers at me. Then the dog begins to growl at him so he takes his arm away. Rover never liked Graham . . . come to that, he never really liked my sister either. Dachshunds have *some* taste.

'Well, I think she's let herself and the whole family down,' says the smug Graham, who must have put on a good couple of stone and a couple more chins since I last saw him.

'Do you?' I say sarcastically. 'Well, I'm sure she'd never have done it if she thought she was going to upset you.'

'W–W–We're trying our best to keep it from G–G–Graham's parents,' sobs Zoe. 'I don't know what sort of f–f–family they'll think I come from.'

Everything she says seems almost designed to make me come out with something meaner than before. It really isn't my fault.

'Listen, you selfish cow,' I yell. 'This is about Mum and Dad, not you or Graham's bloody parents. You haven't even asked how Dad's coping, or whether Mum's happy or if she's even all right. All you're worried about is how it affects you and Mr Blobby here.'

'Now look, I won't have you talking to me and my wife like that,' says Graham, eyeing the snarling Rover nervously. 'Can't you see you've upset her?'

'I tell you what will upset her – and what's going to happen if you two don't piss off back to your crappy little friends and play mothers and fathers somewhere else. Mum and Dad will be much better off if everyone gives them a chance and leaves them to sort things out for themselves. Now sod off.'

There are certain times when just saying something can put right years of frustration. I suppose I've wanted an excuse to tell those two what I thought of them from the beginning. Amen!

Thanks, Ma!

Scene 14

Northbridge High Street.
Thursday 5.00 p.m.

ACTION:

I'm feeling slightly peculiar. I've just left home and I'm on my way to the High Street to meet Mum at the shop and I'm suddenly all sort of nervous. It's just occurred to me that I've never really had a proper conversation with my mum – or my dad come to that – and I'm not sure I know how to do it. I suppose I've got to pretend she's not just my mother, but a normal person, like anyone else. Merlin was right – until I saw her kissing Chloe's dad in the car park, I'd never even thought about her being a woman.

I'd definitely prefer *not* to think about sex. Sometimes I used to try to imagine her and Dad actually doing it, but the idea was so yucky I had to empty my brain pretty quick. But why is that? Why, for instance, can I quite easily imagine Merlin's mum and dad doing it but not mine? Weird. To put my mind at rest, I decided ages ago that my parents only ever did it twice. Just to have babies – a bit like animals do. Which accounts for me and Zoe.

What's even more off the wall is that it's easier to imagine my mum doing it with Chloe's dad than with my dad. What's that all about? I wonder if it's something to do with me being the *result* of my parents doing it – it sort of makes me part of the whole thing, I suppose. Funny, I've never thought of that before either. I still have problems with the idea that I was actually once *inside* my mother, and that I sucked her breasts and ghastly stuff like that.

These are things I haven't talked about with anyone – even Merlin. Perhaps I'm a bit ashamed about my embarrassment. I mean, Merlin laughs about his parents bonking all the time, and he's always going on about when he walked in on them and watched while they were actually at it . . . but I can't see the funny side. To be honest, it's such a long time since I heard any noises coming from my parents' bedroom (apart from my old man snoring) that I guess they've given up. Perhaps that's the whole problem. Perhaps that's what Mum meant when she talked about her and Dad not trying any more.

I can't think about this stuff any more. Here's me, having never gone all the way with anyone and wondering what it actually feels like, and my mum actually *leaving* my dad possibly because it's come to an end. Can it really be that good? Can it actually feel better than – say – snogging Jade Labardia? These days I'm imagining just about everyone at it – uncles, aunties, schoolteachers, politicians, dinner-ladies, you name it. My current puzzle is, what causes people to *stop* doing it?

Suddenly, I'm walking down Northbridge High Street staring at all the old people shopping. Do they still do it, I wonder? If they don't, when did they decide not to? I read once that Pablo Picasso, the famous artist, was still having kids at eighty or something. If that's the case, all this lot could still be at it. Is that a gross thought or is that a gross thought? All those old wrinkly bodies . . . I can't even go there.

I reach the ladies' clothes shop my mum works in and peer through the window. There she is, talking to a customer, smiling and happy and seeming to have not a care in the world. I stand for a while just watching her *not* being my mum but just a person doing a job. She looks *so* not like my mum – so self-assured and . . . . I feel like I almost want to cry. Perhaps she's not only given up on Dad, but, in a way, me as well. Perhaps she's fed up with her whole life at Onslow Drive – Dad, me, Rover, Tweetie and all.

She catches me watching her, waves and beckons me inside.

'Hello, Joe darling.' Then she introduces me to her customer. 'This is Mrs Wilkinson. Her son Scott's at your school. Do you know him?'

The lady looks quite small and gentle. Scott Wilkinson's a right thug from Year Eleven.

'I, er, – don't think so,' I say hesitantly.

'Oh, that's funny, he says he's a friend of yours,' the lady says. 'I hear you're about to be a TV personality.'

It's interesting whenever anyone does anything slightly out of the ordinary, everyone reckons they're his or her mate.

'You didn't mention that, Joe,' Mum says. 'Was it what you did last week . . . ?'

'Sorry, Mum, Merlin got a phone call from the telly people. I, er, didn't really get the chance to tell you.'

Bloody Merlin couldn't keep a secret if his life depended on it. Mrs Wilkinson gives us a strange, why-wouldn't-a-son-mention-to-his-mother-that-he-might-be-going-on-television? look.

Mum comes to the rescue. 'Oh, we were out all day yesterday, and I missed Joe this morning.'

Mum closes the shop and we walk round to the Red Dragon on Northbridge Green. I hope and pray the barman doesn't recognise me, or talk to me even. I sometimes come here with Merlin, when we're feeling brave and we've managed to get a lager or two.

'What would you like Joe – a Coke?'

'To tell the truth, I could die for a lager,' I nearly say – but think better of it.

'Or would you prefer a lager?'

Mum and I both giggle.

'Now, Joe, what's this television thing all about?' Mum asks as soon as we sit down.

'Oh, it's just that Merlin got a call from the people who make that awful programme *Whatzit*, saying that a whole load of kids rang in saying they thought what we did was brilliant. They all apparently hate the two kids who present it.'

'I suppose they are pretty ghastly, but there was no excu–'

'They said they wanted us to come in,' I cut in, 'to talk about a new idea they've got. They've been looking for people to introduce this sort of arts programme for kids – well, kids a bit younger than me and Merlin.'

'Golly, Joe, you on telly regularly? Do you think you'll be able to do it?'

'That's the problem, Mum. I'm not sure that I want to. Merlin's flying around like a flippin' movie star, but the whole thing gives me the willies.'

'That Mrs Wilkinson, the one in the shop, told me that Merlin's telling everyone he's homosexual – is that right?'

'I practically told him that first, Mum.'

'How did you know? Oh Joe, you haven't been . . .'

'Don't be daft, Mum,' I interrupt. 'I think you might have seen some clues by now if I was gay.'

'Poor Merlin. What's he going to do?'

'Why "*poor* Merlin"?' I ask.

'Well, won't he have to see someone?'

'Bloody hell, Mum, it's not a disease. You don't catch it from loo seats.'

'Yes, but it's not very nice, is it? What about his poor parents?'

'What about them? Look, Mum, there's a lot of it about. Blimey, there's a couple down the road.'

'That's different. They've always been gay.'

I sometimes wonder what planet my mother lives on.

'Look, Mum, I don't really think we came here to talk about Merlin. I want to know what's happening between you and Dad.'

Mum runs her finger round the top of her gin and tonic and looks really sad.

'Joe darling, haven't you ever wondered about us, me and your dad? What we're really like?'

'I was just thinking about that earlier. I don't think I've ever seen you as real people. Just Mum and Dad.'

Mum looks serious for a bit.

'Look, I'll try and put what's happened as simply as I can. As you know, I was forty last year, and that's a very big thing for a woman. It's a time when you start to reassess everything.'

'Like what?'

'Mostly, I started to wonder if I was still attractive. That must sound silly to you at your age. The trouble with your dad and me is that – a bit like you just said about how you think about us – we just stopped seeing each other as anything apart from a husband or wife.'

'But that's what you are, aren't you?'

'Yes, Joe, but I had allowed myself to forget that I'm a person outside that. It might have escaped everyone's notice, but I'm actually a woman – not just your dad's wife or your mother – but a living, breathing, emotional and, as everyone seems to have forgotten, *thinking* woman.'

I begin to feel guilty. 'So how does he . . . ?'

'Sorry, darling, let me continue. I started to look into the future and the idea was too depressing. Without going into too much detail, your father and I stopped – how shall I say – *sleeping* together, a couple of years ago. It wasn't just his fault. I suppose I didn't really want to either. He didn't fancy me any more and I didn't fancy him. It was only when I found a pile of girlie magazines in his shed that I realised how bad things had really become.'

'Did you *ever* really fancy Dad?' I ask incredulously.

'I know it might seem funny to you, but when I first met him, I thought he was the funniest, sexiest man I had ever met.'

'Who, DAD? Blimey!' I almost shout it. A couple of oldies on the next table even turn around.

'Look,' she continues in a quiet voice, 'he wasn't always like he is now. There was a time when he couldn't leave me alone. I won't go into it, but we were passionately in love. The trouble is, sex can often become routine, just like cooking supper or walking the dog.'

I think of Rover's antics in the park and nearly make a joke, but stop myself just in time.

'Are you finding this embarrassing?'

I think about it for a second and realise I'm actually not. 'No, Mum, carry on.'

'. . . Anyway, we both started to make excuses for not doing it – headaches, too much on our minds, too tired, you name it. And I thought your dad had just lost interest in sex.'

'Until you found the magazines,' I say.

'Until I found the magazines. When I looked through them and saw all those beautiful, and even not-so-beautiful, girls, I realised that he was now living his sex life in his head – like a fantasy.'

Boy, do I know how that feels, I want to say. I've been doing *that* for ages.

'I felt old and unattractive and past it . . .' she adds.

'Mum, you're not any of those things, honest,' I venture.

'. . . and then I met Gerald. I knew right from the start what sort of a man he was, but I didn't really care. He said really nice things about the way I looked. He laughed when I made silly jokes. He asked me questions about how I felt about things. He even told me he thought I was sexy. In other words, he saw the other me – not just Mrs Derby of 39 Onslow Drive.'

At first my gut feeling is that I want to go round and punch Chloe's dad's lights out, but then I slowly begin to realise what she's saying.

'Is that when you started to dress up when you went out?'

'At least *someone* noticed. It was like I was a teenager again. Suddenly everything became alive. It was like I'd been living in a black-and-white film, and all of a sudden it was colour. I would have gone anywhere with him.'

'Did you love him?'

'I really thought I did, but I was completely blind.'

I know only too well how that feels. I thought I loved Lucy and would love her forever and look what happened there.

'So, he was lying about all those things,' I say, and instantly regret it.

'No, no, no! Not at all, Joe. I really believe he did find me sexy and attractive and funny, but he had no balls. Sorry, Joe, you've never heard me talk like this, have you?'

'It's all right, Mum, I actually quite like it,' I say – and mean it.

She goes on. 'To me it didn't matter, and still doesn't matter, that he stayed with his wife. I will always be grateful to him. He gave me back my spirit. Do you see what I mean?'

'I think so. It's just that . . . it's all a bit of a surprise hearing it.'

'So, now I'm out in the open, I've got to carry on. I don't need another man – not straight away anyway – I want to enjoy being an individual person and not just half of something else.'

'So what about Dad?'

'What *about* Dad?'

'Well, what's he going to do?'

'It's up to him. He can either carry on with his shed and fantasy girlfriends or get a life. I know this sounds really hard, darling, but it's not my problem. I told him everything about Gerald – *everything* – and about how he made me feel.'

'Could you ever feel for Dad like you once did?'

It feels really strange asking my mother stuff like this. It's almost as if *I'm* looking after *her*.

'I don't think so, Joe . . . sorry. I don't reckon I can ever go back. I can't ever imagine your father changing enough to be interesting enough for the new me.'

Just as I'm about to jump to Dad's defence, I take a good look at her and see what she means. Everything about her looks younger and fresher. She's got rid of the grown-up-housewife haircut, shortened her skirt a couple of inches and even undone the top couple of buttons of her sweater. It's funny, I'd noticed a few fashion magazines hanging around the house and didn't think anything about it. Now I realise that her make-up's more like on the models in the pictures – more positive and in-your-face . . . well, in *her* face. Christ, I even reckon if she stood next to my horrible sister Zoe, you'd have a hard time working out who was older.

Scene 15

My house.
Thursday 7.30 p.m.

ACTION:

I'm lying in my dear old kingdom with my second-in-command, trying to make sense out of what my mum has just told me. I wish we'd had that talk a couple of years ago. I might have understood both of them a bit better. It's dead funny – they've wasted all that energy telling me what to do and where I'm going wrong, but never bothered to look at themselves. Actually, it's not *that* funny, is it? It looks as if it's too bloody late.

Mum's all right. She seems to have gone through a complete change and is looking forward. But what about Dad? Is there any hope for him? I know it seems odd after all the terrible things I've said about him, but I can't help feeling sorry for the poor old bloke. There's his wife out there, looking dead cool and all excited about her new life and there's him, stuck downstairs watching telly in his brown corduroys and grey cardigan, just as he always has . . . only all on his own. He must be feeling gutted at the moment. He might not actually have fancied Mum any more, but it doesn't mean he didn't want her around.

I go downstairs and see him sitting at the dining table with a packet of frozen fish fingers and a tin of baked beans, reading the instructions. He looks tired and old and very, very sad.

'Hello, Joe, how are you doing? Did you see your mother?'

'Yeah, Dad, we went to the Red Dragon, just round from her shop.'

'Is she all right? Has she got all she needs?'

'She told me everything, Dad. About you and her.'

'Oh, I see. I bet she said some rotten things about me.'

'You probably won't believe this, Dad, but not *one*.'

He looks a little brighter. I don't mention that she didn't actually say anything nice about him either.

'How do you mean?'

'She more or less said it was both your faults.'

'That's rich. I didn't have the affair.'

'She said you'd both stopped trying.'

'Oh . . . I see.'

He looks very embarrassed. He obviously doesn't like talking about this sort of thing. It doesn't stop me, though.

'She said you and she had stopped seeing each other as real people and that you took each other for granted.'

Dad looks down at the tin of beans and sighs.

'Did she say whether she would ever come back?' he eventually asks.

'She said she didn't think so.'

'What if I were to change?' he asks, without a trace of optimism.

'She said she thought you could never change enough.'

'And there's the new bloke,' he adds gloomily.

'No, there isn't. It's over, apparently. She thinks he's useless.'

'So, she might as well come back when she's had enough time to realise what she's left behi . . .'

'Dad,' I break in despairingly, 'I really don't think you're reading this plot very well at all. It wasn't so much that she was crazy about him, it was more that she was pissed off with you.'

Dad slumps back in the chair and puts his head in his hands.

'So what do I do? I can't carry on like this.'

'You could try to be the sort of bloke women like Mum might fancy. Even if she doesn't come back, someone else might.'

'. . . and how would I do that?' he asks miserably.

'Well, you could start by wearing clothes that don't make you look like Mr Bean.'

I can hardly believe I just said that. An expression of anger flashes across his face . . . and then subsides.

'What? You mean jeans and trainers and things?'

'No, Dad, that would be stupid. You aren't a jeansie sort of bloke.'

'I just wear the sort of stuff I've always worn.'

'There's your answer. You've just got to get out more.'

There's a ring at the front door. Dad goes to get it. I listen to the voices and they seem to be getting a bit cross. Next thing, I hear Dad shouting and the door slamming. He strides back into the kitchen looking like he's about to kill someone.

'As if I haven't got more important things to worry about than that.'

'Than what Dad? Who was that?'

'It was that Mr Smail from down the road. His wife's the one that breeds those spotty dogs – Dalmatians.'

Mrs Smail is quite well-known for her Dalmatians. Two years ago she got runner-up to best of breed at Crufts with one of her bitches. The stupid thing was called 'Autumn Sunshine Over Catford' or something equally pants. Now they've extended their house out the back and seem to be making quite a lot of dosh churning out puppies.

'What did he want?' I ask. 'He sounded a bit pissed off.'

'As if I haven't enough on my plate without his most valuable champion giving birth.'

'What do you . . .'

Before I finish, I suddenly begin to see what he means.

'He said he thinks our Rover did it. He said he dug a hole under his back fence and got into the garden.'

When he hears his name, Rover looks up inquisitively from his basket, thinking it's time for a walk, but then shrinks back as we both stare at him crossly. I, for one, reckon it would be an acrobatic feat for someone as short as him to get up on . . . well, you know what I mean.

'Did he actually *see* him in his flipping garden?' I ask.

'That's what I said,' says Dad. 'He reckons he didn't need to. He'd seen him hanging around.'

'Course he bloody does. He can't just accuse poor Rover like that. That's libel or defamation of character or something – isn't it?'

'I said that too, but then he shoved this tiny puppy at me. I've got to admit, it looks just like Rover with longer legs and spots. He went on about having nine others just like it. He then said this could cost him a few thousand quid in lost puppy sales.'

I look over to my best friend's basket.

'Rover,' I ask sternly, 'is this true?'

Rover slinks out of the room, tail between his legs. I really don't think we need to keep this case open any longer, as Sherlock Holmes might have said to Doctor Watson. To be honest, I don't think this is the first time this sort of thing has happened. I see quite a lot of young dogs in the park that bear an uncanny resemblance to my second-in-command.

Rover is my own personal dog – bought for me by Mum and Dad on my eighth birthday. Unfortunately, he was a prezzie, so I had no choice about what make he was. If it had been down to me, I'd probably have chosen a Rottweiler or a Doberman or something that would have scared my mates. But Dad, being the mean bloke that he is, got a special deal. Rover was the runt of a litter of wire-haired dachshunds owned by a chap at his work, so he was practically being given away. Wire-haired dachshunds are basically standard sausage dogs with stubbly grey beards on their faces (and bodies).

Not that I'm complaining, honest! Rover's turned out to be as cool as a dog can be. He'll fight or shag anything that moves. If Rover was a bloke, he'd be a super-stud – the sort of guy *Sunday Sport* would write features about. Despite his substandard stature, he seems to have no trouble at all with his bitches (sorry, but that *is* the correct word for lady dogs). His chat-up routine is direct if nothing else – one quick sniff and he's away. No flowers, chocolates or candlelit suppers for him. The funny thing is that the whole female canine population of Northbridge seems to rather go for his less-than-formal approach – big, small, pedigree, mutt, young or old . . . I wish it was that easy for me.

'So what's the bloke up the road going to do?' I ask.

'He said he's going to see if he can take it further.'

'That's all right,' I giggle, 'Rover's skint. They can't get blood out of a stone – or a dachshund.'

'Yeah, but I'm not a bloody dachshund, am I?' moans Dad. 'What if he sues me for negligence?'

'Why, because Rover wasn't wearing a condom?'

Dad looks at me slightly annoyed . . . at first. And then begins to smile – the first smile I've seen for ages, poor sod. I meet his eye and he begins to laugh quietly. The next thing we know, we're both literally crying with laughter and hugging each other for dear life.

Good old Rover!

Scene 16

The Northbridge shopping precinct.
Saturday 11.07 a.m.

ACTION:

I can hardly believe it, but since that evening when my dad and I fell about laughing over Rover shagging the neighbour's dog, we've been getting along really well. It's as if Mum leaving has brought us together. It's now just a question of staying alive. For a start, motivated by the prospect of approaching starvation without her around, we bought a cookery-for-idiots book.

It works like this. I choose the recipe in the morning and tell Dad what to buy. He gets the grub during his lunch hour and brings it back after work. Then, together, we follow the instructions to the letter. It's rather fab. The food not only comes out looking like it does in the pictures, but it tastes pretty good too.

On Thursday, we both ran out of clean clothes and found ourselves staring blankly at the washing machine, thinking what the hell do all those dials and knobs do and where are you supposed to put the soap powder? We can't even open the bloody door! Luckily, Dad found the instruction book in the cupboard over the sink and we studied it for about half an hour before even touching it. And hey presto! To our amazement, it worked a treat.

Ironing was a bit more tricky, but, can you believe it,

I turned out to be a right wizard at it and was even able to show my dad how. We both agreed that women have been going on far too long about nothing to make us men feel guilty. Most of it, when you come right down to it, is just basic common sense, we decided. I did, however, humbly suggest that maybe the point wasn't how difficult each thing was, on a scale of one to ten, but the fact that women (or should I say my mum) always had to do just about everything. And some of them (again, like Mum) had to do it after they'd come home from *full-time* day jobs. When I mentioned that Merlin's mum and dad seem to share everything around the house, Dad looked a bit sheepish.

Dad and I are in Men in Vogue in the precinct, the object being to try to get him kitted out in something that makes him look slightly less like Norman Normal from Normalton-on-Sea. It took hours of gentle persuasion to get him to even consider that a new look might do him good, but he eventually came around. To be honest, I don't think he's even seen a shop like this before. Most of his clothes came from department store sales and, as he told me, some of them were bought by my mum.

I look at him and can't begin to think what might suit him. Luckily, anything's going to be better than what he usually wears . . . especially at weekends . . . especially *this* weekend! He's not too fat or too short or anything, so there's no reason why clothes shouldn't fit all right and even look quite good. Steering my father past all the naff stuff, however, is like leading a drunk through an off-licence. Everything even remotely naff or dull catches his eye.

'Ah, that looks like the sort of thing,' he says, stroking a snot-coloured, cable-knit cardigan.

'Walk on, Dad,' I say, 'that's what they dribble on in old people's homes.'

'That's very reasonable for a blazer,' he says, inspecting the label of one that's identical to the one he's wearing.

We eventually leave with a couple of pairs of quite cool chino-style trousers, half a dozen good quality white T-shirts, some extra-large sweatshirts and a pair of soft brown leather deck shoes. I make him wear some of his purchases into the street. I have to say he looks completely different.

'Thank God that's all over,' he says. 'Can we go back now?'

I take another good look at him and then dive in at the deep end.

'Dad, I know this a might seem a bit cheeky, but I think you should have your hair cut properly.'

He looks amazed. At the moment his is the sort of hair you see on old-time cigarette cards of footballers – short at the back and sides, and long and greasy and combed back on the top.

'What's the matter with my hair?' he splutters. 'It's always been like this.'

'Look, Dad, you can't keep going to that awful barber

by the station. They should be called "Apaches' not "Chris's" – they scalp you as soon as they look at you.'

'But I've been going there for twenty years. They all know me by my first name.'

'Yeah, but they've only got one haircut – the one that make you look like you're in *Dad's Army*.'

I steer him, protesting, towards Clippers, a hairdresser's in the High Street that does women and men. It's almost next door to where Mum works. I can tell being so close to her is making him really twitchy.

'We can't go in there,' he says, staring into the rather poncy salon. 'They're all girls.'

Poor old Dad reluctantly edges into Clippers and luckily – or so I thought – the only bloke in the place comes trotting up.

'Oh hello, gentlemen, I'm Martin. Have you an appointment?' he asks in a voice camper than a row of pink tents.

Dad looks relieved. 'Er, no,' he says, 'sorry to have bothered you. We were just passing. I'll make an appointment some other time.'

'Oh, that's all right,' Martin laughs theatrically, 'we're not that busy for a Saturday morning. I could slip you in now if you want.' He smiles knowingly at me with an I-could-slip-you-in-too look.

'Does your friend want me to sort him out after?' he enquires cheekily, like I'm deaf and dumb. 'He's going a bit dark at the roots,' he says, referring to my bleached hair.

'He's not my friend,' says Dad, almost crossly. 'He's my son – and he doesn't.'

Dad looks terrified as Martin leads him self-consciously past the backs of the women and towards the vacant chair at the end of the salon. I have to sit patiently flicking through the magazines spread all over the place like a rash. I don't often look at women's magazines, especially now my sister Zoe's gone, but I only need to pick up one to remember how full of junk they are. Endless articles about how to make your boobs bigger or your bum smaller, or how to satisfy your man in bed by wearing stupid underwear, or how to cook him a meal that'll give him a hard on . . . you know the sort of bollocks.

Then there are the photos of long, gorgeous waif-like birds who'd look good wearing the front-room curtains, modelling clothes bound to turn out bloody awful on the average girl in the street. And what about the ludicrous horoscopes, promising dim Debbies from Dagenham a wild affair with a Brad Pitt lookalike next month? Pants, I say.

'Blimey,' says Dad, when he eventually comes back, 'he charged me twenty quid for that. It only a *fiver* at Chris's.'

'Yeah,' I reply, 'but at Chris's you only got what you paid for.'

Forget the clothes – the hair makes all the difference. Martin has cut Dad's hair really well – fairly short all over and flattish on top. Even the old man admits he looks ten years younger. It really is surprising how underneath his long-term, deeply unattractive disguise, he really isn't bad looking. I feel like I'm responsible for one of those makeovers they have in the magazines I've just been looking at. As he's leaving, he catches sight of himself in the full-length mirror by the till and is slightly taken aback. And he even straightens his back and walks a little taller as he hits the street.

'There's only one thing left,' I say.

'There *isn't* anything left,' he replies nervously, 'unless you're going to make me wear false teeth.'

'It's your glasses, Dad.'

I've always thought they made him look like a short-sighted child molester. 'People wear smaller frames now. You can even get ones you can stamp on without them breaking.'

'Why would I want to do that?' he asks, missing the point entirely.

They've just opened one of those new places that can fit the lenses on the spot and have the finished glasses ready in an hour or so. I make Dad try on nearly every pair, until we finally agree (well, *I* finally agree) on a pair that look quite cool. Opticians or optometrists, or whatever they're called now always seem to be full of pictures of good-looking models, who probably wouldn't be seen dead in glasses in real life pretending they actually look better. Personally, I can't see how walking around with two magnifying glasses stuck to your nose, can ever be anything but weird (unless they're shades).

Having said all that, Dad agrees his new ones are a great improvement and, as he strolls out of the store, I notice he's got a slight spring in his step.

After we've had a Big Mac and done Sainsbury's, Dad and I drop back in to pick up the glasses.

We have to pass Mum's shop on the way back to the car park, and unfortunately, just as we're opposite the window, she looks up and waves. I wave back and Dad waves nervously too, but she gives him a strange look, like she doesn't know who he is. Blimey, I say to myself, am I *that* good?

Then, when we eventually get home, Rover, the stupid mutt, bares his teeth and growls menacingly as if I've arrived with a complete stranger.

Scene 17

My house.
Saturday 2.15 p.m.

ACTION:

When we get back, Dad moves around furtively, catching sight of himself in mirrors and trying on different combinations of his new clothes. It's all rather sad, I think. I'm sure he wishes he could go out and show them off, but the poor guy's got nowhere to go and no one to see when he gets there. It starts me thinking again about marriage. I just can't see the point. You spend day after day, week after week, year after year with the person you once promised to love and cherish for ever, until you practically know what they're going to say next. Which is OK if you like that sort of thing, but then something happens, like they leave you or die or something and you look round only to find you're completely alone with no friends. And it's bad enough for people of my dad's age, but what about when you're old and wrinkly? It's too depressing to think about . . . so I won't.

Tonight I've got a proper date with Chloe – the first one – and I'm a bit nervous. I would have liked to talk about it with my new mate (Dad), but, 1) we're not quite ready for that, and 2) it's with the daughter of the bloke that's just had it off with his wife. This is the sort of thing that's only supposed to happen in soaps.

Anyway, Chloe wants to see *Moulin Rouge*, because it's all about dancing, which is making me even more nervous. Much as I want to go out with her, the idea of a musical – *any* musical – fills me with unbridled dread. Also I'm *not* one of those blokes who gets the hots for Nicole Kidman. She always seems a bit pale and insipid to me – and worse . . . Australian. What am I talking about? Kylie's Australian and I could get off on her singing and dancing to the 'Trooping the Colour'.

Burger-Babe.
10.30 p.m.

If there was any doubt about Chloe's intentions with regard to me, they soon disappeared in the darkness of the back row of the Ritz Cinema. Any idea I might have had that she was a sweet little innocent ballet dancer couldn't have been more wrong. I'd hardly sat down before her hand was fondling my arm, and then my leg, then wheedling its way into my . . . er, popcorn. If I'm to be honest, I can't remember very much of the movie, except there was a lot of jumping around in big frilly knickers, and a load of not very good pop songs which they managed to make worse by singing badly.

When it's over, we go across the road to Burger-Babe where I first met Chloe on that ill-fated evening when Lucy introduced her to Merlin.

The trouble with a smallish suburb like Northbridge is that you are always in danger of running into people you know. I suppose that'll be the biggest advantage of having a car – at least you can play away from home (and on the back seats).

Tonight turns out to be no exception. Just as we sit down, the next person I see coming through the door is Lucy with her parents and some guy I've never seen before. They've obviously been to the same film. Talk about embarrassing.

Chloe doesn't bat an eyelid.

'Hi Luce,' she calls, 'have you been to the movies?'

Lucy looks well put out at seeing Chloe with me, but can't really say much, because *she's* with another bloke.

'Oh, hi Chloe, hi Joe. Where's Merlin?'

She obviously wants to embarrass me, thinking that Chloe is Merlin's girlfriend.

'Over here!'

We all whip around to see Merlin, falling about laughing behind a potted palm with . . . would you believe it, Martin, the bloke who cut my dad's hair. We all wave.

'Blimey,' I whisper, 'this is like The Last bloody Supper. Who's going to turn up next? Jesus?'

'How about your mum with my dad,' giggles Chloe quietly, 'or your dad with my mum.'

'Or your dad with my dad,' I say.

Lucy and her parents exchange a bunch of pleasant, if somewhat boring, banter with me and Chloe and then sit down at the table across the way. I can feel Lucy's eyes boring into the back of my neck.

'I recognise that bloke with Lucy,' whispers Chloe. 'He works at the fitness centre she and her mother go to.'

'I wonder if he knows which one he's supposed to be out with,' I murmur cattily.

'What about Merlin?' she says. 'He didn't waste any time. Anyway, how did that camp guy with Merlin know you? Is there something you want to tell me, Joe?'

'No, I took my dad out last week and gave him bit of a makeover . . . new clothes, new glasses, new hair. He looked really good.'

'You really are a sweetheart, aren't you?' Chloe coos, touching my arm. 'Not many guys would have done that for their dad.'

'I really feel sorry for him, actually. He's in a sort of vacuum.'

'What do you mean?'

'Well, ever since he married my mum, it's as if he's given up paying any attention to what other people are wearing. It's like he's a walking time-capsule. Everything sort of stopped developing in the early eighties.'

'I think that's rather sweet, really. It's better than my old man who's obsessed by what he looks like,' Chloe says gloomily.

'He pulled my mum, though, didn't he?' I reply sadly.

'It's just the contrast, Joe. I bet your dad's worth twice mine, when it comes down to faithfulness.'

'Of course, but that doesn't make him sexy, does it?'

'Not like his little boy,' says Chloe, fluttering her long eyelashes in a dead obvious way.

'I don't know about you,' I say, 'but the back of my neck's burning from the Lucy laser.'

'Yeah, I noticed. She hasn't taken her eyes off us.'

'Don't you mind?'

'Why should I? I care more about what Merlin thinks than Lucy. She's not exactly the most faithful person who ever drew breath. Do you want to move tables, Joe?'

'No, it'd look too obvious. Anyway, we've done nothing to feel bad about. As long as Merlin's all right, that's all that matters.'

'He looks to be very all right,' giggles Chloe, glancing over to Merlin's table.

'Anyway,' I say, teasingly, 'we're only friends, aren't we?'

Chloe puts her hand on my leg again and smiles. 'I can be as friendly as you like, Joe.'

I once saw this old movie called *Tom Jones*, where the hero, a proper ladies' man, was having supper with this really well-endowed wench. It was set in the eighteenth century or something, and the woman was wearing one of those frocks they used to wear, where their boobs practically flop out whenever they lean forward. When they were near the end of the meal they both took ripe pears from the fruit bowl and began to peel them. It's a dead famous piece of direction. The way they ate the pears left the audience in no doubt about what was really on their mind, and what they were going to get up to later. I know hamburgers aren't the same, and that

Burger-Babe bears little resemblance to an old, candle-lit coaching inn, but I can honestly say that at this moment food isn't really on my mind, or Chloe's either, given the way she's looking at me.

Luckily, just as we're about to go into a full snog, ignoring everyone else, Merlin and Martin come to our table.

'Hi Joe and Chlo, this is Martin. I think you've met before.'

Martin breaks in. 'Yeah, this morning. I cut his dad's hair. He looked quite cute by the time I'd finished with him.'

'I don't think I'd ever use the word cute about my dad,' I say. 'But he did look a darn sight better. Thanks.'

'I can't believe it,' says Merlin. 'Your dad's the straightest bloke I've ever met. He makes the Royal Family look like swingers.'

'Oh, I don't know,' Martin breaks in, 'I thought he was dressed quite well for a bloke of his age.'

'That's only because Joe made him buy new clothes,' Chloe interjects.

'What's going on, Joe?' asks Merlin. 'Since when have you bothered about what your dad looked like?'

'I was just telling Chloe. I was feeling a bit sorry for him. Mum's left him, and he's got hardly any friends. He just watches TV or sits in his shed, making his bloody models.'

'Poor bloke. Meantime your mum's having a high old time. I saw her in Jangles the other night with a bunch of people. She looked really fab. Tell you what – my mum and dad are having one of their do's in a few weeks' time. Why don't I get them to invite him?'

'He'd never come,' I say. 'He'd be too nervous. Especially among your parents' mates.'

'He'd come with you, though, wouldn't he? I'm going to have a few people round too.'

'Look, I really don–'

'Aw, come on, Joe,' interrupts Chloe. 'He might quite like it.'

'Yeah,' said Merlin. 'You never know what might happen. I seem to remember you saying he was quite funny at Chloe's parents' do.'

'I'd forgotten that. He had me falling about at one point. He was taking the piss like mad.'

'I hope he wasn't taking the piss out of my dancing,' says Chloe. 'He told me he liked it.'

'No, it was just the music. He thought it was pants.'

'I bet he didn't use that word,' says Merlin.

The walk to Chloe's house is best not reported on in great detail. When we get to the park, she drags me into the shelter and leaps on me. She really is another Jade. When she snogs, she really snogs. So hard, in fact, I hardly grab a chance to draw breath. Unlike Jade, however, who is warm and exotic and almost sort of languid, Chloe is fast and exciting and urgent. She makes you feel as if you're the only person she's ever kissed in her life – ever *wanted* to kiss, even. But the best thing about Chloe is that she and I never run out of conversation. I remember those tedious walks home with Lucy, who seemed to be rendered speechless, the minute you veered off the subject of clothes or who Robbie Williams was currently going out with. As for Jade, I never was able to be with her long enough to find out (even though I still wouldn't mind).

The other best thing about Chloe is that she doesn't seem to want to smother me (apart from in the park shelter). She seems perfectly happy for me to go off and do my thing with Merlin or whoever, and see me whenever we've both got time. I must say that for a first date, it really couldn't have gone much better.

Scene 18

The television studios.
Saturday (one week later) 10.30 a.m.

ACTION:

It's Saturday morning and Merlin and I are waiting to be called in to see the TV people. To be really honest, over the past week I've been getting into more and more of a state. The meeting's been looming for a couple of weeks and the closer it got, the more I realised I couldn't get out of it, and the worse my state got. I suppose, if I tell the absolute truth, I *do* know my place, and it certainly isn't in front of a television camera. It's different for Merlin. He gets a real buzz from being the centre of attention, and he's good at it. *I* reckon it's a bit more cool to be in the background. The trouble is, I don't want to let him down. Jeez, what if they insist it's both of us or nothing?

Chloe's been brilliant. I talk to her nearly every night after school. She says you can't run your life worrying about other people, that if I don't want to do it, I should tell Merlin and be done with it. The trouble is, I'm even more scared of doing that than going on the flipping telly.

The girl at the reception desk comes over and leads us to a really flash office with a view overlooking the river Thames. Two men and a woman are sitting on big white sofas drinking coffee and they all stand up as we come into the room.

'Ah, there you are,' says an older man, 'Merlin and Joe, isn't it? My name's Robert Shelton and I've just been brought in to run Children's Programming. Can I introduce you to one of our producers, Johnny McCoy, and our production secretary, Sophie Hughes? I hope you found us all right. Please sit down.'

We take the third sofa while the woman sorts us out with something to drink.

'I don't know how much you know about why we've asked you here,' he goes on, 'but we're at the very early stages of an idea, and as we're hardly in the first flush of youth – as you've probably noticed – we'd appreciate your input.'

The guy called Johnny stands up, lights a ciggy and walks over to the window.

'We might be wrong,' he says, 'but we got the impression from your performance the other week, that *Whatzit* might not be your favourite show.'

'It's crap,' says Merlin. 'I hate all that sort of jumping about stuff. I think they make fools of the audience.'

The older man smiles. 'It's taken us a while, but we tend to agree with you. We've been looking for another way of doing it for a long time. What we know is that we want kids to be taken seriously, but not so seriously that the programme isn't "fun".'

(I hate that word 'fun'. Only old people use it when talking about things that young people like doing.)

It's Johnny the producer's turn to speak.

'It was only when we saw your less-than-reverent

performance last Saturday week that it all clicked. You two cut through all the twaddle right away and the audience, at home and in the studio, absolutely loved it. We've got loads of letters and emails to prove it.'

'We didn't do it on purpose,' says Merlin, 'it was just when they said they hadn't even seen the film we were there to talk about, that we went kind of bonkers.'

'They always seem to bring everything down to a really stupid level,' I add. 'There are lots of kids out there that think that's all rubbish.'

'So it seems,' says the woman, who I couldn't help noticing had really good legs. 'We would like to do a pilot of the sort of show that has never been done before. A sort of popular arts programme, featuring young people, just like yourselves, who are actually doing real things.'

'It could get a bit nerdy,' says Merlin. 'You could end up having a load of stamp-collectors and trainspotters.'

Johnny giggles and looks approvingly at the other two.

'You've got it in one. That's exactly what we have to avoid. Somehow we've got to find the sort of people who really take what they're doing seriously, but are not anoraks. We're pretty sure they're out there, but the big question is, can we find them?'

'You wouldn't make it *too* arty, would you?' I say. 'That would make the kids run a mile.'

'Not at all,' says Johnny. 'We want them to be doing real things.'

'What sort of "real things"?' asks Merlin looking suspicious.

'Well, let's see . . . Maybe we could find someone who plays an instrument brilliantly . . . not a prodigy, but just a kid who plays in his bedroom. Or someone who's a great cook, or maybe someone who makes their own clothes, or films, like you and Joe did.'

'Did you see it?' Merlin interrupts looking slightly menacing.

The three of them laugh.

'You're not catching us out this time,' says Johnny. 'We watched it a couple of times. It's really funny.'

'You could invite the best website designers,' I suggest.

'Or video game players,' Merlin adds.

'Or someone who's really done a number decorating their bedroom,' I say, 'like a sort of set design.' I'm thinking of Jade's Arabian palace and Merlin's dungeon.

'I think you've got the picture,' says Robert, the boss man. 'The question is, how to present it?'

'We wondered if you two would like to have a bash,' says Johnny, '. . . do a pilot – and see how it goes.'

I'm just about to voice my objection when Merlin gives me a kick on the ankle.

'We'd love to,' he says, glaring at me. 'Have you got a script?'

'We'd like to talk about that too.'

'What about money?' asks Merlin.

Jesus, I can't believe he came straight out with that. I can't help admiring his nerve, though. I would probably have done it for free (if I'd actually wanted to do it) without even thinking about being paid.

Johnny, the producer, speaks first. 'We've got a budget for the pilot, so we'd be able to give you a straight fee. If it goes ahead, then obviously we'd be talking to your agent.'

'We haven't . . .' I begin to say.

'That sounds fine,' says Merlin, speaking right over me, 'I just wanted to get things straight.'

'You'll need a couple of researchers,' says Sophie. 'They'll work on your instructions, and find the sort of people we want to feature.'

'What about music?' asks Merlin. 'Can we get away from poncy girl and boy bands?'

'That might be more difficult,' says Johnny. 'We have to fight the ratings battle to get the advertising.'

'You could have a mixture of chart people and the best of the young bands that are still struggling to get seen,' I put in.

I suddenly have a thought – a thought that might get me out of this.

'What about school? How are we going to do this and go to school?'

'We've already thought of that,' says Johnny. 'This comes up quite a lot, as you can imagine. We reckon that with our help you can do it in two days a week . . . Saturday and one weekday. We'll be able to square that with your head teacher. But let's start with the pilot and see where it goes.'

Merlin and I look at each other in disbelief.

* * *

Leaving the studios, I feel half happy and half terrified. I realise, as soon as I'm in the lift, that if I was going to say anything about not wanting to be a presenter, I should have done it a long time ago. By joining in the discussion, I must have more or less convinced them I was up for it. Me and my big mouth!

Scene 19

My house.
Saturday 12.44 a.m.

ACTION:

When I get home, I tell Dad all about what's just happened. He seems genuinely interested, but I can tell he's got something else on his mind. I ask him what's up and he goes to the dresser and hands me a letter. It reads:

Gardner, Smithers and Partners, Solicitors
Henley House
Marlborough Court
London W1 6AG

23rd June 2002

Dear Mr Derby,

We have recently been instructed by our client, Mr T Smail of 75 Onslow Drive, Northbridge Middlesex. He submits that on or around April 1st this year, your dog, a wire-haired dachshund, did impregnate his wife's champion Dalmatian bitch, Sunrise Sally of the Cairngorms, causing it to give birth to ten puppies of no commercial value whatsoever. This means, effectively, that the bitch in question will miss a season and that as a result, as the puppies could be expected to sell for around £400 each, he will be out of pocket by as much as £4000.

We have seen photographs of said puppies and there seems to be little doubt that your dog is responsible. Mr Smail submits that you did negligently and wilfully let your dog roam the streets and that the said dog broke into the rear yard of his wife's, Mrs Smail's, breeding establishment. He will therefore be looking to you for the reparation of his loss.

Please inform us, at your earliest convenience, as to your response to our client's allegations.

Dad reads the letter again and turns to me, looking well fed-up.

'What shall I do? I don't have four grand to fork out every time Rover gets randy. It's funny, just after Smail came round that time I rang my solicitor, and he said they'd never get away with it in a million years. He said no solicitor would even take it on. Looks like he was wrong.'

'It's nonsense, Dad. They can't do it. Anyway, they still can't prove it was Rover. There might have been another wayward dachshund in the area.'

'What if old Smail pays for a DNA test?'

'Do they do them for dogs? You've got me there . . . but they can't take Rover to court. It's bonkers. Why don't you ring your solicitor again, Dad?'

'He won't be there on a Saturday. I'll have to wait until Monday.'

Suddenly a thought strikes me. 'Wait a minute!' I say. 'What was the date on that letter? The date that they said that Rover gave that Dalmatian one.'

'Hang on,' he says, skimming through the letter. 'It says on or around April 1st.'

'As far as I know, dogs are pregnant for just over three months. It's only June now. That makes it impossible.'

'Wait a minute,' says Dad, 'April the 1st, April Fool's Day. You don't think this could be a wind up?'

'Let's check the postmark. Did you keep the envelope?'

'It should be on the top of the rubbish. Let me get it.'

He hands me the crumpled envelope.

'The postmark says Woodfield. Isn't that where your office is, Dad?'

'Blimey, Joe, you should be a bloody detective.'

'Did you tell the blokes at work all about this?'

'You bet I did. They've all been telling me to expect the worst.'

'Mystery over, Dad. You've been well and truly set up. Just to make sure I'll ring directory enquiries and see if there really is a solicitors called Gardner, Smithers and Partners in London.'

I ring directory enquiries only to find that no such solicitors are listed, there or anywhere else. Dad looks both furious and relieved, but eventually sees the funny side of it.

'You wait till I see them on Monday,' he says, with a vicious gleam in his eye.

'Come on, Dad, there must be a way to get them back. Isn't there some way you can turn the tables? Make them squirm a bit?'

'Can you think of anything?'

I love things like this. They appeal to my devious nature. I think for a bit and then have a brilliantly timed brainwave.

'I know – on Monday, why don't you tell them about the letter and say you were so angry you had Rover put down. That'll make them feel really awful for starters.'

Rover looks up at the mention of his name, but presumably has no idea what we're talking about.

'Yeah, and I can say I had to borrow the money at huge interest, to pay the bloke back. I can say I really didn't want to go to court, because I didn't want to incur extra costs not knowing what the outcome would be.'

'This is getting really good. With a bit of luck they'll be so embarrassed they'll have a whip-round.'

'What for? To buy us a new dog? We could have one of the puppies.'

'If they weren't so ugly,' I say with a giggle.

We both howl with laughter, upsetting Rover, who has no idea that he's at the centre of all this attention.

When we've calmed down, I say, 'Dad, I've been meaning to talk to you about something.'

'Fire away.'

'You know my friend Merlin.'

'Course I do. He's a queer now, isn't he?'

I ignore the less than caring comment. 'Apart from that, his mum and dad are having a party in a few weeks' time, and they've asked if you'd like to come along.'

'They're a bit weird, aren't they, the Labardias? I saw them at that dreadful concert. It's not really my . . .'

'Oh come on, Dad,' I break in, 'you know you've got to get out more. It's a chance to show off your new image.'

'But they smoke dope and all that, don't they?'

I haven't heard puff called dope for years, but I keep my cool and soldier on.

'There'll be all sorts of people there, Dad. I won't leave you alone, I promise. You never know you might meet someone nice.'

He suddenly looks all sad and small. 'I don't want another woman, Joe. I just want your mum to come back.'

'I know, Dad, but you've got to get a life in case she doesn't. You can't just hide in that shed.'

'With my ten ugly puppies . . . I know you're right, son. Thanks, I'll think about it.'

Up in my kingdom, I lie on the bed to have a good worry. On top of all this stuff with Mum and Dad, I can't get this flipping telly business off my mind. Part of me would quite like to be famous, of course, with loads of money, flash girlfriends and all that. But I just don't think it's my style somehow. I reckon, to be a personality and to do it well, you've really got to want it bad – like Robbie Williams or Gerry Halliwell. Mind you, I think people like that are dead uncool. It's almost as if they only really exist when they're in the public eye, and much as they make a fuss about being snooped on, they make a bigger fuss when they're not. And I don't suppose there's anything more pathetic than being an *ex*-famous person. I still reckon my favourite thing would be to be a renowned film director. Not really well-known, because my photos aren't in the tabloid papers all the time, but because of the little flashes of real glory every time I win an award.

'And now, ladies and gentlemen, the award for this year's best picture goes to the legendary director, Joe Derby.'

I can just see myself, doing the classic 'Who me? Surely not. I'm so completely surprised' reaction, then walking up to the podium in a cool suit and dark glasses, where some gorgeous woman with practically nothing on is waiting to kiss me. My speech would go something like this:

'Thank you so much, ladies and gentlemen, for bestowing yet another honour on me. Normally I would be expected to thank my producer, the production staff and everybody that goes to make a film right down to the tea lady. I won't, however, because I reckon I did this film all on my own, and all the others simply got in my way. [Pause for uproarious laughter.] As for my dear wife, I can honestly say that without her support this film would probably have been a damn sight better. [Pause for more laughter.] Seriously, though, film-making is a team effort and I am just a very small cog in the great machine. Thank you all so much and enjoy the rest of your evening.'

I then walk off stage to thunderous applause, from an audience who think I'm the best thing since sliced bread.

The Kingdom of Joe Derby.
Saturday (two weeks later) 6.27 p.m.

ACTION:

Ever since Merlin announced to the world that he was gay on national television, he seems to have become camper and camper. It's got to the point where he's hardly the Merlin I know and love (well, like) anymore. God knows what the telly people will think the next time they meet him. I had a word with Jade and she says she thinks it's probably just a phase, like when you get a new bike and can't bear not to ride it all the time. I found the comparison a bit strange, but I suppose I get the point. Anyway, I flipping well hope she's right.

It's not all bad, though. While Merlin and I drift gradually apart, Chloe and I drift gradually together. We now talk every night, and I've even been known to dash round to meet her train on her way home from ballet school. Distinctly uncool, but hey, who cares? It's great – I'm too busy being her mate to keep having to ask myself whether I still fancy her or not, like I had to with Lucy. I really, really, *really* like her.

'Chloe,' I ask her, 'can I pick your enormous brain? You know this TV thing? Well, I've thought it all through till my head hurts, and I now know for absolute sure that I don't want to go ahead with it.'

'Then don't!' she replies. 'That'll be five quid for the advice.'

'Ha, very ha! The trouble is, I still can't think of a way of getting out of it without pissing Merlin off big-time. He still thinks they want both of us or nothing.'

'What, like Ant and Dec?'

'Not quite, but that sort of thing.'

'Have you tried talking to him, like I suggested?'

'I tried, but if I even mention not doing it, he goes all gay and arsy.'

Chloe goes quiet for a while, stops walking and then turns to face me. 'Sounds like I'll have to talk to him again, Joe . . . he really listens to me. I even think he's a bit scared of me, if you want the truth.'

'Would you really Chlo?'

'Only if you're really nice to me on Saturday night at his parents' party.'

'I'll be as nice as you bloody want, if you get a result. Do you know, this is the first time I've ever been to a party with an actual girlfriend.' (Did I just say that?) 'I usually only end up finding them or losing them at parties.'

'Well, don't try any funny business on Saturday. I'll be watching you like a hawk. I know what you're like, Joseph Derby, especially with Jade around.'

Oh hell, I think to myself, I hadn't thought of that! I've got to know Jade Labardia pretty well now, and a situation like this – me arriving with a girlfriend is just up her street.

* * *

132

Lying in bed, I start worrying about my mum and dad again. I know I always used to go on and on about how unpleasant it was when they were here together, but given the option, I'd give anything to get things back as they were. And poor old Dad, although he tries like mad to shed a lifetime of serial boringness, carries on like a little dazed bunny rabbit, mooning around the house, reminding himself of Mum constantly. I've been thinking a lot about it recently and have come to a couple of monumental conclusions: 1) to be a rebel, like me, you've got to have something to rebel against. Now Mum's gone, the fun's gone out of it; 2) everything I said about cleaning and washing and cooking being easy was complete and utter bollocks. After a couple of weeks, Dad and I have found ourselves sliding back into our dreadful old ways – buying crap, easy-to-prepare food, wearing the same underwear till it practically begs to go to the washing basket, and being late for just about everything. Come back, Mum, all is forgiven.

Having said that, Dad *did* briefly snap out of his remarkable boringness and do something pretty hilarious. When he got to the office, the Monday after he got the letter from the phantom solicitors, he told his workmates that I was heartbroken about Rover being put down, and that he was already struggling to raise the money to pay the first instalment of the loan he took for the fine. The moment he brought it up, apparently, he knew for sure they'd done it, and he could see from their guilty faces they were really struggling to decide whether to tell him it was all a joke.

After work, a small delegation came up to him and confessed all, offering to make some recompense for the upset it must have caused. Dad then told them that he'd been winding them up and that the dog was alive and well. I think he should have been awarded a good few points for having that lot over a barrel.

He's finally agreed to come to Merlin's mum and dad's party, too, provided I don't leave him on his own and he can go when he wants (sometimes I wonder who's the father and who's the son in this relationship). Now that he's stopped being paranoid, he sounds almost as if he's looking forward to it. He's also really got into this clothes thing. Even without my help, he's been out buying completely new gear, right down to new pants and socks. Most of it, I have to confess, really isn't that bad. He's also been talking about borrowing some money (genuinely this time) to buy a half-decent car. But I'm not quite sure why. Maybe it's to impress the ladies, but I don't think so. Unless there's someone I don't know about at work, he seems completely uninterested in other women.

So, I suppose he's coming around, really. He might *not* be the most boring dad in the world after all.

I have another trick up my sleeve, but if it backfires, I'll be up to my neck in the old proverbial poo, and that's for sure.

Scene 21

Merlin's dungeon.
Friday 5.20 p.m.

ACTION:

Merlin finally seems to have come to terms with the idea that I don't want to be a presenter. Chloe, true to her promise, sat him down and told him how it was and he accepted it . . . grudgingly. But I agreed to go along to the meetings in case there's some other role I can play.

It turns out that they really would prefer a boy and a girl to present the show, so they might well have been giving one of us (probably me) the heave-ho anyway. I told Merlin that they could save some money because they'd get both with him, anyway, but he didn't seem to find it very funny.

He asks if I'll help him with ideas, and that he'll pay me out of what he gets, when he gets it. This, of course, sounds just about the biz to me, though I'd prefer to get a proper job in my own right, like researching or deciding who to have on.

In our first meeting at his place I suggest to him that he should play the whole gay thing down. If they were looking for a would-be panto dame, I said, they'd have asked for one.

'Ah, my dearest Joe. For once, I might have to agree with you . . . So,' he says, 'do we know anyone that we could use in the pilot?'

I think for a bit.

'What about that guy at school?' I say. 'The red-haired kid that plays the fiddle in his dad's Irish band.'

'What, all that diddly-diddly music?' he replies camply. 'Pleeease! It's not very "now" is it?'

'OK then, you could do a piece about Chloe and her dance school. I should think a lot of girls would be really into that.'

'And blokes,' replies Merlin with a misplaced leer, 'but aren't we being a bit too local? Remember we can have anyone we want, from anywhere in Britain.'

'Yeah, right, but how do we find them?'

'Well, it'll be all right once we're up and running,' says Merlin. 'We'll be able to ask on each show for people to phone in. It's just the first one that's tricky.'

'You could do a thing on Jade's whacky room, like we said at the meeting. It'd be great. I bet lots of kids would like to deck out their rooms like film sets or something. She could show them how to do it.'

'Yeah you're right, we needn't even let on she's my sister.'

'. . . and if you're stuck, you could do a short piece on our film. That's what started it all off, isn't it? It's only the introduction programme.'

Merlin writes down all our ideas and we take them to meet the programme producers. They say they like the idea of me helping with ideas and they even say that if the show goes ahead, they'll include me as a writer in the budget – cool or what?

The idea of featuring Jade's room works a treat. So we record a little sequence using Merlin's dad's flash video recorder, in which Merlin does a rather daft but quite funny interview with her.

The telly people really get off on the idea of kids doing up their own rooms, and think it could be a regular feature. But they're more interested in the *girl* in the room. Although they'd seen flashes of Jade in *La Maison Doom*, they hadn't seen her live sort of thing. They think the rather spiky rap between brother and sister really works, and tell Merlin to ask her if she'd like to try co-presenting instead of me. Jade, who's almost as big a show-off as her brother, goes barmy at the idea and says that she's thinking of a special way of thanking me.

If it's what I think it is, I hope she doesn't plan it for Saturday night. In fact, to be honest, I find myself not really wanting to get involved with her any more while Chloe's around. Blimey, Joey boy, what does *that* mean?

Scene 22

My house.
Saturday 7.30 p.m.

ACTION:

Dad and I are getting ready to go to the Labardias' party. He comes down the stairs wearing the black trousers we bought the other week, a black polo-shirt and a dark blue jacket.

'Does this look all right, Joe?'

'Better than all right, Dad. You look cool.'

Then I catch the shoes – light brown lace-ups. 'You'll have to do something about those, though, Dad.'

'What? The shoes? What's the matter with them?'

'They don't go. Haven't you got anything black?'

'Only the ones I wear to work.'

'Anything would look better than those, Dad.'

The black shoes do look much better and apart from the slight funereal slant, Dad and I could possibly be the best-looking father-and-son act on the block. My dad's a classic case of good looks having as much to do with the way you present yourself as anything else.

The Labardia parties are particularly good value, because there are always two of them – one for us youngsters (usually held in Merlin's dungeon) and one for the geriatrics. This time I've promised to hang around in oldsville, so my dad doesn't panic. Dad's never visited the Labardia house, and I've been wondering what the poor old bloke will make of it.

As soon as the front door opens and he catches sight of the stuffed bear in the front hall, wearing the shiny pink cowboy hat, I can tell he's uncomfortable.

'Joe darling,' says Merlin's mum, 'how lovely of you to come. And this must be your father . . . Derek, isn't it? I don't think we've actually ever met.'

'Er, yes . . .' says Dad, staring in awe at her cavernous cleavage, 'I mean, no, we haven't. I, er, saw them – er, sorry – you, at that music thing, but we never spoke. But thank you for inviting me. I'm afraid I haven't been getting out that much lately.'

You haven't been getting *anything* much lately, I nearly say, but think better of it.

'Well, we'll soon make up for that,' says Merlin's mum, looking around at some of the guests in the main room. 'Let me introduce you to Amanda le Fraine. She's an actress friend of mine. She'll look after you.'

I look over and see a rather frightening-looking lady with long black hair pouring herself a drink.

'Don't leave me, for Christ's sake, Joe,' whispers Dad as he's led across the room.

Poor old Dad. Talk about chucking him in at the deep end. The nearest he ever got to talking to anyone remotely to do with the arts was at Chloe's parents' party – and look what happened there.

'Ah, Amanda darling,' says Merlin's mum, 'let me

introduce you to Derek Derby and his son, Joe. Joe made that wonderful film with our Merlin.'

I doubt whether Dad has ever seen a woman like this, let alone spoken to one.

'Er . . . nice to meet you,' he says. 'Would I have seen you on the telly?'

She laughs louder than strictly necessary. 'Oh no, I'm afraid I'm purely theatre, darling. Why, are you in television yourself?'

Dad coughs and looks fairly helpless.

'No, I'm a quantity surveyor, actually.'

'How absolutely divine. I don't think I've ever met one. What exactly do you do?'

For one second the old man perks up and it almost looks as if he's going to tell her. Bad move number 314B, Pa! Dad's one of those people who, if he knows anything about what he's talking about – which is rare – will use five hundred words when a few would do.

He catches me frowning and amazingly gets the message.

'Oh, it's nothing very interesting. It's more or less brick counting.'

Amanda le Fraine giggles affectedly and grabs my old man's arm. 'I'm sure you're teasing. I'm sure it's really complicated and that you must be *reeea*lly clever.'

'Oh well,' says Dad, beginning to relax, 'I suppose not everyone could do it.'

'Not everyone would *want* to,' I say under my breath.

My attention wanders as Dad can't resist telling the

striking but suspiciously dumb woman the ins and outs of the exotic and spine-tingling world of quantity surveying.

Oh no . . . shit! I suddenly spot Chloe's dad and mum. As much as I love Merlin's parents, subtlety and tact aren't exactly their strongest point. But when I talked it over with Chloe, we both agreed that even *they* wouldn't invite both my dad and the man who's been shagging his wife. How wrong can you be! I start feeling nervous. This is going to make my devious little plan even more tricky.

Then I spot Chloe, looking really cool in a dead straight, long black dress and high heels. She doesn't normally wear heels, being a ballet dancer and all that, but when she does, she looks really tall and fab and sophisticated. She's chatting to an already slightly drunk Merlin's dad, whose expression leaves nothing at all to the imagination. Short of actually dribbling, he does little to hide who he'd jump on if there was a power cut. Come to that, I wouldn't put it past the old letch to organise one. She stares at me with one of those wide-eyed, eyebrows raised, if-you-don't-rescue-me-soon-Joe-Derby-I'm-going-to-knee-him-in-the-balls looks.

'Hi, Mr Labardia,' I say. 'Hi, Chlo. Have you been here long?'

'About fifteen years,' Merlin's dad jumps in, laughing. 'I live here, as you know. I've just been chatting up young Chloe. I tell you, Joe, great girls like this are wasted on the young. What they really needs is age and experience.'

Tony Labardia is one of the only people I know who

could get away with comments like that. I think it's because he's generally so up-front and honest. Unlike most other people, he always says whatever comes into his head and then laughs it off without a further thought. Just like Merlin. It's dead funny – people hardly ever get cross with him. When he sees Chloe's reaction to me, however, he realises there's nothing for him here and sidles off, to find fresh game presumably.

'Shall we go upstairs and see what's happening at Merlin's?' Chloe asks.

I look across the room where my dad's now surrounded by *three* women, all presumably receiving a crash course in quantity surveying. I feel it's safe to leave him for a while.

'I must be back down here for about nine-thirty,' I say.

'Why's that, Joe?'

'It's a bit complicated, I'll tell you later.'

Oh dear, oh dear. When Merlin decides to do or be something, he certainly doesn't do it by halves. As our eyes get accustomed to the candlelit gloom, we notice that there are more boys than girls in Merlin's dungeon, some of whom I've never seen before. Several of them are from my school, including the blond guy from the Sixth Form, who was sent home for having his nipples pierced.

Despite not knowing that Merlin even knew these guys, I've a fairly good idea what they've all got in common. It's a bit like birds. Take hedge sparrows and ordinary sparrows – they all look the same to us, but they all seem to know the difference between them when it's home time. Actually it's nothing like that, really.

'Isn't it funny,' Chloe says quietly, 'all the grown-ups downstairs are on their feet jigging around to music, and up here everyone's slouching around in the dark.'

'I suppose the adults have done all the slouching around in the dark they're ever likely to do.'

'Now they just do it in flash cars,' Chloe says gloomily, knowing that I'll get what she's on about.

Merlin spots us and leaves his little bunch of admirers.

'Joseph darling – and dear Chloe – how wonderful to see you. Do come in, we're having cocktails.'

'Can I have a beer, Merlin?' Chloe says. 'I think I've seen enough pretentiousness downstairs.'

'Meeow!' giggles Merlin. 'How's about you Joe? Fancy a Penis colada?'

'No thanks, Merlin,' I say, skilfully ignoring the crude joke, 'I'll have a beer too, if it's not too ordinary.'

Someone taps my shoulder.

'Joe sweetie!'

Oh no! It's Jade, wearing a dress that shouldn't be allowed out, '. . . and Chloe. Have you two just arrived?'

Chloe looks positively frosty. Girls are so like that. If anyone even slightly edges in on what they think is their territory, you can practically see their claws coming out.

'Hi Jade,' I say. 'What's going on?'

'Apart from Merlin turning his room into a gay club, nothing much. It's a good job Sky and I invited some straight blokes, or there'd be no one to play with.'

It's just at that point I spot Lucy glowering at me and Chloe from across the room. This really isn't turning out to be my evening.

At twenty past nine I suddenly realise I've got to go downstairs.

'So, what's happening, Joe?' whispers Chloe. 'Tell me what you're up to.'

'I'll explain in a minute. Let's go downstairs. God, I hope I've done the right thing.'

When we get back downstairs, things are beginning to warm up. Chloe's dad is drooling all over Amanda What's-her-name, who, ironically, keeps throwing pleading glances towards my dad to rescue her. Dad looks like he's having quite a good time, dancing (Dad's DANCING!) cheek-to-cheek with a rather glam woman with big hair and a backless (and, for all I know, frontless) dress. Well done, Dad.

Despite all the noise, I hear the doorbell. Oh well, Joey boy, here we go. This could either be the very best thing you've ever done in your life . . . or the very worst!

I get to the front door just as Merlin's mum is opening it.

'Barbara!' she cries. 'How absolutely wonderful to see you. I didn't know you . . .'

'I hope you didn't mind me asking Mum along,' I

break in. 'It's just that I never get to see her these days. We only speak on the phone.'

Mum looks absolutely brill. The Keep Fit classes are obviously working a treat, and almost to prove it, she's wearing really tight-fitting black jeans and a black sparkly top.

'I hope you don't mind me coming, Sheila, but I've rather lost touch with everyone since . . . since – well, *you* know. I would have been here earlier, but we were stock-taking after the shop closed and then I had to go home . . .'

I wince when I hear her say 'home'. That *used* to be where I lived.

'Of course we don't mind! It's wonderful to see you. Please come through. You'll never guess who else is here . . .'

To tell the truth, I don't know whether she's going to say my dad or Chloe's, but I don't want to find out, so I jump in.

'Hi Mum. You look fab. Can I get you something to drink? You know Chloe, don't you?'

Chloe, bless her, who has every reason to hate my mum, rushes forward and gives her a big kiss.

'I always wanted to talk to you,' she says quietly, 'if only to apologise for my dad. He's here by the way.'

'I guessed so,' says Mum gloomily. 'They see quite a lot of the Labardias, I've heard. I wanted to come along, just to show everyone that I'm not someone that can be pushed to one side.'

Her eyes scan the room, but go right past Dad who

she plainly doesn't recognise . . . again. I don't suppose the tarty-looking woman in his arms helps. Anyway, I bet it wouldn't occur to her that he'd come to a thing like this.

'Brilliant,' says Chloe. 'Come on, Joe, get your mum a drink. I bet she's dying of thirst.'

As I weave through the dancers, I look back to see Chloe and my mum falling about laughing together. Chloe's got to be just about the best thing going. So far she hasn't done one thing that hasn't knocked me out.

As I get to the bar, I notice that Chloe's father has spotted Mum and has gone ever so slightly pale. Then I turn to where I last saw Dad dancing. He's standing completely motionless, mouth open, staring at his long-lost wife, with the backless woman hanging on for dear life. Jeez, I think, what in hell's name's going to happen now?

I rush back to where Mum's standing with Chloe, but it's too late. She's spotted Dad pushing his way across the room.

'Hello, Barbara. You look terrific. I didn't know you were coming.'

'D–Derek, I hardly recognised you . . . the hair and the new glasses . . . and you've lost weight. . . and where did those clothes come from? . . . I had no idea you were going to be here either. Look, I'll go if you want. I don't want you to feel awkward.'

'No, I'll go. I've been here a while. Look, I'm really sorry. This is pure coincidence really.'

They suddenly both turn to look at me and I give one of my famous angelic smiles, as if I know nothing about it. There's a short silence while it all sinks in and then Chloe starts giggling.

'You little bugger,' Mum eventually says to me. 'You set this whole thing up. What were you thinking of, Joe?'

'It's just that I can't stand you not at least being friends – it's bloody stupid and I bloody hate it. You're always going on about me for acting like a kid. Now it's my turn to accuse you two of doing exactly the same.'

Chloe squeezes my hand and all of a sudden I feel it's going to be all right.

Mum and Dad start chatting slowly and awkwardly at first, but gradually, as they relax and even start to enjoy each other's company, I feel it's safe to leave them alone. Chloe and I drift away.

'So *that's* what you were up to, Joe,' she says. 'You're either mad or the bravest person I know. What if she'd turned up with someone?'

'God, I never thought of that. Flipping hell, that would have been ghastly. Talk about rubbing my dad's nose in it even more.'

'Well, I think you're brilliant. I think they should be proud of you. Tell you what, let's get another drink.'

Chloe and I end up at the edge of the Labardias' huge garden. I feel an overwhelming urge to say something about how I feel. I can't bear the idea that she might think that I see her as just another girl. In American movies, kids do poncy things like give each other rings and stuff to prove their commitment, but we're far more cool over here, so I decide to speak.

'Chloe,' I say, when we're alone in the little summer house, 'I think I like you more than any girl I've ever been out with . . . To tell the truth, I don't know how I'd have handled this Mum-and-Dad business without you around.'

'I think you've changed towards them, Joe. I think it's made you see them as real people and not just your boring old parents. I bet whatever happens now, you'll all get on much better. By doing what you did, and saying what you just said to them, you've become like *their* dad for a bit. I wish I could do that with my bloody parents.'

I then say something I've never said in my life on account of it being so uncool.

'Chloe, what do you think about me?'

Chloe put her finger to my lips and then said slowly, and very sexily, 'Close the door, Joe, and I'll show you.'

Scene 23

Looking back.

ACTION:

It's about three weeks since the party and everything's going scarily well. So well, in fact, that I'm beginning to worry that it won't last. Typical me, eh? Worried about having nothing to worry about.

Anyway, soon after Dad came over to speak to Mum at the Labardias' party, Chloe's mother caught Chloe's old man giving his mobile number to that Amanda le Fraine woman. Chloe thinks this could well be it. Her mother had said, after the affair with my mum, that it would be down the old divorce court if she ever caught him at it again. Chloe said that, despite everything, she realised she actually liked her dad more than her mum, and that the only reason he's been messing around so much is because her mother's such an old cow. She reckoned if he ditched her and got a place on his own, he'd settle down and find someone more suitable. As long as it's not *my* mum, I told her.

Dad came up to me when Mum went off to the loo and gave me a real man-to-man hug. He said that he'd suspected that I was up to something, but reckoned it was some sort of set-up with Merlin's mum to find a partner for the ghastly le Fraine woman. He said he was really proud of me and joked that if anything did ever happen between him and Mum again, it would all be my fault.

Mum also grabbed me at the end of the party and suggested that I go into the counselling business when leave school. I bloody well hope she was joking. She told me that when she'd seen the back of my dad dancing with the glamorous woman in the backless dress, before she knew who he was, she was thinking how cool he looked. She said that people don't become more interesting just by wearing better clothes, but that she thought that Dad had finally realised how much he'd let his life slip and how much he'd taken things for granted. Better still, she said that when he told the story of Rover shagging the neighbour's dog, she remembered how funny he could be. I watched them talking and realised that whatever happens in the future, there was a real chance they'd remain mates, which was all I'd ever asked.

They've been kind of dating for the last few weeks, and they're beginning to look really easy together – easier than I can remember. In one of our long late-night phone chats Mum had told me that over the last month she'd really began to miss him in a funny sort of way, and she couldn't think why. Maybe that was it. Maybe it was Dad's off-the-wall sense of humour she missed. I really don't know if they'll get back together, but it won't be for lack of my dad trying.

He hasn't stopped either. Not only is he beginning to completely re-design the house (he hasn't been in the shed for weeks), but he's even leasing one of those little MG convertibles through his company. The only thing is, unfortunately, he's started wearing a baseball cap when the top's down. God, I hope he doesn't drive too far down the road to Middle-Aged Trendsville. I might have created a worse monster than the one I had before. I might have to have a word with him, in fact.

Back to the party. Jade managed to corner me when I went to fetch some drinks to take out into the garden and said she thought Chloe was a lucky girl. She said that she'd always fancied me, but that she'd always known I was very much a one-girl sort of guy. She said that she and her sister were like greedy kids in a sweet-shop and always had been. As soon as they have their hands on one thing, they're already looking across the counter at something else. It was dead noisy, but I'm pretty sure she whispered that once I'd finally gone all the way, I could always call her to brush up on technique. I was left wondering whether she meant practical or aural? (or maybe *oral*?) Still, eh!

Merlin came down to earth long enough to say that his proposals for the programme had gone down very well and that they'd be shooting the pilot as soon as all the technical stuff had been sorted out. I wondered whether I'd feel jealous now that I wasn't going to be a TV star, but found I didn't give a damn when it came down to it.

Talking about Merlin, he's taken to his newfound gaydom like a duck to water. Not that I've ever met a gay duck, as far as I know. The funny thing is, he seems to have become a magnet for all the girls at school, which even he finds a bit odd. Maybe they feel safer with him now.

So that's about it. What went on in the summer house at the end of the garden on the night of the party is my little secret.

Now, where did I put Jade's number?

Also available from Piccadilly Press, by
JOHN FARMAN

'Joseph, are you in there? It's me, your mother.'

Damn, I thought it might be that Jennifer Lopez again; she usually calls round about this time for a quick snog.

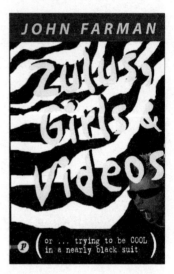

- **ZULUS** I always think my life's a bit like living in that old film *Zulu* – you know, the one where Michael Caine (me) and a bunch of rather hot British soldiers (Rover) are holding this garrison fort in Africa somewhere against thousands of ever-so-cross natives (my family).

- **GIRLS** This is really sad. One minute my head's full of the gorgeous, sexy Jade, and whether I might stand a chance with her after all, and the next, I'm thinking of dear sweet Lucy. Jade–Lucy, Lucy–Jade, I just can't get my brain straight.

- **VIDEOS** I'm a complete cinema junkie – a filmoholic – a movie maniac – a video voyeur, you name it. I don't know why, but all I ever think about is films (oh yes – and girls).

"Lively, witty text by a diverting writer." *Publishing News*

In the same series: *Merlin, Movies and Lucy Something*
Sequins, Stardom and Chloe's Dad

If you would like more information about books available from Piccadilly Press and how to order them, please contact us at:

Piccadilly Press Ltd.
5 Castle Road
London
NW1 8PR

Tel: 020 7267 4492
Fax: 020 7267 4493

Feel free to visit our website at
www.piccadillypress.co.uk